SECOND EDITION - FIRST PRINTING

September 17, 2001

Copyright 2001 by Kevin Howard. No part may be reproduced without the permission of the Author or the Publisher:

ISBN# 0-9679378-0-9

Printed
in the
USA

Published by
Home-Boy Productions
6128 So. Pilgrim St.
Seattle, Washington 98118

Letters to My Lover

Chapter 1	Gotta Dance	Pg. 7
Chapter 2	Initial Thoughts	Pg. 12
Chapter 3	The First Letters	Pg. 15
Chapter 4	The Wedding	Pg. 25
Chapter 5	Bumping Heads	Pg. 29
Chapter 6	The Big House	Pg. 30
Chapter 7	On the Road to Europe	Pg. 32
Chapter 8	The Maintenance Man	Pg. 44
Chapter 9	The Boat Trip	Pg. 47
Chapter 10	The First Trip to Portland	Pg. 53
Chapter 11	The Big House – Free Rent	Pg. 57
Chapter 12	Letters Later...	Pg. 60
Chapter 13	The One-Year Anniversary	Pg. 63
Chapter 14	When Does a Dream Become an Obsession?	Pg. 66
Chapter 15	Come Dance with Me	Pg. 67
Chapter 16	Georgia On My Mind	Pg. 68
Chapter 17	Canadian Getaway	Pg. 69
Chapter 18	A Seattle Perspective	Pg. 73
Chapter 19	What do you Think of This Idea?	Pg. 76
Chapter 20	Leaving the Big House	Pg. 77
Chapter 21	Across America Together	Pg. 80
Chapter 22	The New Life Begins	Pg. 81
Chapter 23	A Black Man's Perspective	Pg. 83
Chapter 24	Angela	Pg. 84

Table of Contents

Chapter 25 Still Gotta Dance .... Pg. 85
Chapter 26 Poetry in Motion .... Pg. 88
Chapter 27 It's Hot! .... Pg. 92
Chapter 28 Arnett Howard's Creole Funk Band .... Pg. 92
Chapter 29 I'm Bored .... Pg. 94
Chapter 30 Religion .... Pg. 95
Chapter 31 The Second Year .... Pg. 96
Chapter 32 Friday Night .... Pg. 97
Chapter 33 Sexy Dreams .... Pg. 99
Chapter 34 Perception and Reality .... Pg. 103
Chapter 35 Thoughts of Loneliness .... Pg. 110
Chapter 36 The Man's Dance .... Pg. 111
Chapter 37 I Apologize .... Pg. 113
Chapter 38 Finding Stuff for the Big House .... Pg. 114
Chapter 39 Back in the Great Northwest .... Pg. 115
Chapter 40 Breathless .... Pg. 119
Chapter 41 Let's Take the Plunge! P6. 120
Chapter 42 Paris Bound .... Pg. 122
Chapter 43 We Have Breaking News .... Pg. 126
Chapter 44 Three Weeks Later - Omari's Thoughts .... Pg. 128
Chapter 45 Going Home .... Pg. 131
Chapter 46 Completing the Big House .... Pg. 135
Chapter 47 A New Beginning .... Pg. 136
Chapter 48 Back to Reality .... Pg. 137

There was a young man named Leo Givens
But now there is no more
What Leo thought was H2O
Was H2SO4!

Granddad

Preface

Spring-cleaning season is in high gear and I'm determined to organize some of the "stuff" that's collecting dust around the house. Rummaging through a storage closet, I come across a neatly sealed box, marked *"Letters"*.

Breaking the seal to inspect its contents, I realize the box contains a treasure of memories, in the form of letters, received from a very special friend named Autumn.

Opening the first letter, I begin to read. Soon, I'm reading one letter after another and a flood of memories begin dancing in my head.

Assembling the letters in the sequence in which they were written, I would like to share with you our wonderful tale of love. Our story is told through our letters written to one another and narrated from my perspective.

Sitting beside the box and reading our letters made me realize how strong our love remains to this day and how genuinely grateful I am.

Letters to My Lover

Chapter One
Gotta Dance

I look outside to see what the weather is like and it's a typical Seattle winter evening-dark, raining, and cold. Damn. That's my reaction to the "Seattle sunshine," especially tonight, because I'm dancing in Portland, Oregon. So I say to myself, "Don't let it get you down; dress warm and drink some coffee. Get down there early and take the time to warm up. Let the music flow and dance! Come on, you've done this routine a million times; just get your butt moving." So...

I make the three-hour trip to Portland. By the time I arrive, my body wants to move. Luckily, there's a half-hour to stretch out before the show begins. We're playing in a beautiful theater with a recently remodeled, turn-of-the century décor. The place holds a thousand people and configured so that the audience surrounds the stage. The theater is packed and you can sense the crowd's anticipation.

Lora, our leader, has assembled a large group of musicians and dancers for this particular performance. Beautiful Lora. She's a musician, singer, dancer, and one wicked business manager. She also makes all the costumes and always has the troupe looking as if we've stepped out of the latest fashion magazine. By her appearance, you can never tell she's in her forties. She has an artistic style and grace that enhances everything she touches. Lora wears her hair in braids and always presents herself as a Nubian Queen.

We're a tight troupe. That's probably why we're getting so much work and, to be honest, all this dancing is keeping me in shape.

Dressed in a matching skirt and top, along with a majestic head-wrap, Lora walks to center stage to begin the show. She opens her arms to greet the audience. "Tonight you will experience music and dance from the Shona tribe of Zimbabwe. We believe if you can talk, you can sing and if you can walk, you can dance! We also believe there's no difference between the audience and our

Letters to My Lover

performance. So please feel free to get up and sing and dance with us!"

We're waiting in the back for the show to begin. Little Casanova, my dance partner and "partner in crime" remarks, "Shit man, the audience is ninety percent white, another night of watching a bunch of dead fish flop around!" We all break out laughing! But it's cool, because we're getting paid big time tonight! In fact, these nighttime gigs are pulling in more money than my regular job. Therefore, I can tolerate watching white folks dance offbeat for two hours. (Well, almost!)

Lora signals the rest of the troupe to come on stage. We begin each set in the same way. It's like watching the best sprinters in the world running the hundred-yard dash! Our first beat starts at the top and we never let up! Never! When the audience thinks they have a chance to catch their breath, Lora signals in the dancers, and we put on a visual display that makes your head spin.

During the middle of the first set, it's apparent that something magical is in the air. The African beat is infecting everyone. It's like a wildfire blowing in the wind and in no time at all, the energy in the room is undeniable.

Lora has a way of playing with this intense energy. She can sense and direct it, as if painting a picture. Lora reminds me of a jazz singer, improvising as she goes along, making it feel just right. We know when she flings off her headdress, it's time for her to display her supreme talents as a dancer, and she never fails to amaze us. It's an immense pleasure working with Lora and our repertoire fit any occasion.

The driving rhythms push the music to a fever pitch and white folks are flopping everywhere. An African brother joins us on stage and grabs a drum. Lora looks over the crowd and then glances at me. This is a signal that she wants the men to push the energy level even higher. About this time, I'm thinking to myself, "Boy, I'm going to get tired tonight!"

Now, I'm glad that I've taken the time to get down to Portland early and warm up. Being thirty-five years old and trying to hit some

Gotta Dance

of the same dance moves I did when I was twenty-five, took quite a bit of warming up (and two aspirins)! For my ego's sake, it's important to mention that the other guys I dance with range in age from eight to twenty-five. However, I still have some stuff they can't touch, so they respect "the old man". What made our troupe tight is that we'd been dancing together for so long. We knew each other's moves and sometimes it was fun to improvise as we go along, just to keep things fresh. I keep telling everyone, "Let's pace ourselves, we have all night." Of course, as soon as I say that, Tendi hits a beat so funky it makes you sweat just to listen to it!

One thing I've learned about dancing with younger guys is that you let them go first. They're eager to show their stuff and have energy to burn. Let me tell you a little bit about our troupe…

You'd never know that Little Casanova is Lora's son. He grew up around the music and dancing is natural to him. He's a little guy for his age and even though he's eight (going on thirty), he looks five. He's also a hustler by nature and always eager to learn a new trick. We're cut from the same mold and I acted as his mentor. Little Casanova can dance with the best and has a few original moves of his own. We have routines that we perform, on and off the stage, according to the audience.

Shelton is a big, black, Mandingo-looking brother, straight out of South Africa. He's twenty-five. He could've been a coal miner; he had the right body for it. He knew the boot dances of his native land and mixed rhythms with his dancing. Shelton is one of the smartest brothers I've ever met. He knows more about the United States than most people born here. Shelton always runs and leaps two or three rows into the crowd, then rips off his shirt, flexing his muscles to the rhythm of the music. You hear the women yelling, "Keep going, Baby!" That's my signal to go out and get him. Then, we go into our James Brown routine where he pushes me aside and continues to flex his muscles for the crowd. Shelton is always getting offers from horny women wanting to "drive him home." (Some didn't have cars!)

After Shelton finishes, Tendi walks to center stage and goes

Letters to My Lover

into a drum solo. Tendi's twenty years old, with a musical ear that is truly a gift from The Creator. He masters every instrument that he touches and can recite any song after hearing it only once. Tendi's the musical leader of the group. He composes musical arrangements in his head and teaches the different parts to the members of the band. He's undeniably a young Duke Ellington reincarnated. This guy plays songs within songs for his own amusement while on stage. Tendi and I have a special connection. His musicality flows through me and makes my body move. You can tell Tendi's passion for African music, because when he's finishes his solo, smoke is coming off those drums!

I begin to dance after Tendi takes his bows. I bring a jazzy, African flavor into the mix. After watching these guys push the pace to a frenzy there isn't much left for me to do. Usually, I throw in a few fancy steps and signal the band to stop on a dime. Everything goes from all hell breaking loose, to a screeching halt. These guys make it look like this climax is built up just for me. The truth is, they've danced their butts off, and I'm still fresh. That's what you learn at thirty-five! Now, where are those aspirins?

This night feels special and something unusual is about to occur. It's the end of the second set and Tendi is stoking a fire under the dancers. I look out into this sea of a thousand people and can't resist what I can only now describe as a "mysterious force" directing my eyes toward a certain person.

Usually, I don't allow myself to be distracted. Because, my heart is in the music and it's the music that makes me dance. However, her inviting face distracted me. Her soft brown skin accents distinct facial features. As I notice her beauty, it's as if the music stopped. I glance at Tendi, and he's drumming like crazy, yet I don't hear a sound! I look at the other dancers and their bodies are moving to the beat. My body's dancing, but my focus is on this lady's beautiful face. She's standing in the first row, directly facing the stage. A jubilant smile lights up her face and it's obvious she appreciates the show. I feel compelled to find some way to introduce myself.

The timing is great, because after working this crowd into a near riot, Lora signals us to end the dance and we take our break.

Gotta Dance

(Giving me a chance to suck on the oxygen bottle!)

Let me make something clear. Being a dancer and doing extroverted moves *on stage* doesn't necessarily equate to an extroverted personality *off stage*. In fact, I consider myself a shy person. However, this is different. I wanted to meet this woman. The million-dollar question is, "How do I make the introduction?" I can simply walk up and introduce myself, or, better yet, take little Casanova. All the girls consider him cute; he'll help me.

With little Casanova in tow, we head off in a path that will allow us to intersect with this beautiful lady. Everyone is stopping us along the way, wanting to compliment our show. I see her talking with her girlfriend; she points to us with an inviting look. We make eye contact. I give her a wink, letting my facial expression show my interest in meeting her. She winks back. Soon enough, we meet and she welcomes us with a warm embrace. "Hi, my name is Autumn. You guys are great, and you little man, you're so cute!" (Yeah, right.) The first thing that comes out of little Casanova's mouth is, "Hey lady — he likes you." Casanova slyly laughs, knowing that he's embarrassing me. "Hey, shut up. You don't have to speak for me; I can speak for myself!" I feel myself blush with embarrassment! "I'm sorry, Autumn. Let me introduce myself. My name's Omari. It's a pleasure to meet you."

Little Casanova, knowing that he's much smoother than me in these situations, cracks a little smile, rolls his eyes, and goes into a familiar routine. The women begin to surround him, echoing the same line we've heard a million times. "Hey little man, you're so cute." Next!

Autumn and I continue to talk. I can tell she's far more than a pretty face. Unfortunately, in what seems like a blink of an eye, our conversation, which is becoming more than mere small talk, must end. "Autumn, in this next set we're going to do a special dance, and in the middle of my solo, I'm going to put in a back flip, just for you!" Immediately after uttering that foolish boast, I'm thinking, "When you're thirty-five years old, trying to act like you're twenty years old, it usually spells disaster!" However, Autumn left such an impression on me, I

Letters to My Lover

feel determined to pull out and dust off that old mating ritual, even if it leaves me a hopeless cripple!

To make a long story short, it was a magical night. Our performance was magnificent and our interaction with the audience left everyone wanting for more.

The best event of the evening, which would change the direction of my life, was meeting Autumn. By the course of the evening, we'd exchanged addresses and phone numbers and promised to write one another. One important element of dance is the relationship between space and time. Put in simpler language, I like free and open space, and writing seemed an amicable approach to getting to know such an attractive lady.

This is where our story begins. That night, I made it down to Portland and met Autumn. Little did I know, with that introduction, our lives would never be the same.

Chapter Two
Initial Thoughts...

Omari's initial thoughts:

There's a subtle essence about Autumn that's attractive (besides being female with all of the associated body parts). Physically, Autumn is *strikingly* beautiful. She's athletic and it's obvious she spends time in the gym. Yet, her inner beauty is what intrigues me.

Autumn stands slightly taller than the average woman. She looks to be a mixture of different bloods. Her hair, twisted into short dreads, lends an air of wildness and freedom. Her lips, which are full and round, project a sense of softness. Autumn makes me feel like a purebred bloodhound that has just picked up a fresh scent. Normally, I don't go around comparing myself to "dawgs," yet this attraction provokes some sort of primal instinct.

To get to know Autumn will require making time in an already overloaded schedule. Whom do I remove to find room for my new interest?

Initial Thoughts

Right off the top, Ms. Tanya is a prime candidate. She's a high maintenance girl who is always stressing my wallet. Her predictable routine of ordering the most expensive item on the menu, along with a to-go bag, coupled with requests to subsidize her rent in exchange for some booty is a played-out script. I figure; if I have to pay to get some lovin, let me get a little more variety!

Pursuing Autumn could be as exciting as going fishing when the salmon are running! One good thing about the Great Northwest; you only need to catch one big fish and you're good to go. Maybe it's not proper equating women to fish, but any good angler will tell you that going fishing in uncharted territory can exact a steep price! Well, I've promised to write; maybe that'll give me the chance to extract a bit more information.

After being burnt a few times, I've learned some things about women. I've learned that it's better to wade cautiously into unknown waters, just to see how cold and fast the current's moving. No more diving in headfirst for me! My last, meaningful relationship was going great until that *multiple personalities disorder* intruded upon the scene and stuck around for an extended visit. One day "Sybil" was the loving person I knew, but the next day, "She-Rah, the Princess Warrior" would come riding in on her white stallion, trying to be as much of a man as me. The only thing she didn't try to do was write her name in the snow (if you know what I mean)!

I will admit that women can be a handful. If they're not cynical or neurotic from a prior relationship, they're usually broke because of it. (Hey, I'm the first to admit that dealing with brothers can create a little drama!) The first question I wanna ask a woman these days is, "What's your daily dosage of Prozac?" Another litmus test is to see if she can cook anything besides microwave popcorn. Of course, they get bonus points if they have any credit limits left on the VISA account. (Yes, I'm being cynical! But you get my drift.)

However, I'm gonna keep a positive attitude with Autumn. It takes two to tango and you never know how well you'll dance together until the music starts. So, let's see if this old "dawg" can show some flexibility. Am I willing to show how much of a gentleman I am, by

Letters to My Lover

spending the night (on the couch) just in case her ex-boyfriend gets drunk and tries to make a midnight booty-run. No problem!

Even the name Autumn sounds sexy, and her bright personality left quite an impression. (The look of that booty left one hell of an impression on me!) So here we go. Let's start out easy and move the chess pieces around a bit to see if we can capture this Queen.

Autumn's initial thoughts:

Omari's a good mover and it's always nice to watch a sexy man with powerful hips. (Are his lips as strong?) This guy must make his rounds, because you don't develop moves like that without a lot of practice! I wonder how many females are in his stable. He even tries to throw a little wit and charm in the mix. But, the little man has him beat by a mile!

Omari is a good-looking man, standing six feet tall without an ounce of body fat. I must admit, when the dancers came out wearing nothing but loincloths and I saw that six-pack stomach...uh, uh, uh, a few nasty thoughts swirled through my mind! However, I've been that route before...all body and *no* brains. (Can I get *both* to go, please?) With these guys, it takes about a week to see through the bullshit. Then the beer-guzzling, sports-obsessed, gas-passing slob shows up, plops down on the sofa, scratches his crotch, and acts as if he doesn't want to leave. Still, the bottom line is, "good trade" is hard to come by. So, I'll try to keep an open mind and let him dig his own grave.

It's tough being a modern woman. The last homeless, jobless, lazy bum ran up my credit cards and took off with my VCR as a memento of our loving relationship. I should've sensed something was wrong when he called the same night I gave him my number, begging to drop by for a visit. Okay, maybe I haven't had the best of luck with men, but Omari *does* have nice conversation, a cute butt, and you just can't top a good "Mandingo brother". What else can a modern woman want? I hope he can cook, because the only thing I'm good for is microwave popcorn! (Plus, I can use a little help with my VISA bill!)

Initial Thoughts

  Well, he has my address and phone number. If he's interested (and I hope he is), I'll let him make good on his promise to contact me.

Chapter Three
The First Letters

Dear Autumn,
  On the night we met, I looked outside at a God-forsaken night. It was dark, cold, and wet; a combination that tempts one to stay at home and rent a video. I tried to think of any excuse to get out of dancing. I'm tired. My big toe's killing me. Why should I drive down to Portland? But, after consideration, I knew the hardest part of the battle would be getting there. I also knew if I didn't show up, Lora was going to skin my Black ass. So, I drink a cup of *Starbucks* and off I go into the cold, uninviting night.
  It took a while to warm up, but after listening to those funky drums, maybe I wasn't *ready* to dance, but at least I was *willing*. I remember Lora giving me the signal to get the guys ready to go out there and fire up the house! Halfway through the dance, an irresistible force directed my attention to where you were standing. I can recall the vision as if it were happening now. You're moving to the music and absorbed within the moment. Suddenly, I couldn't hear the music and could only concentrate on you.
  I remember thinking, "What a beautiful woman, (I wonder how neurotic she is)." (Joke!) From then on, I couldn't take my eyes off you! You looked at me and winked—my heart nearly jumped out of my chest and I suspected this could be the start of something very nice. I said to myself, "Before the night is over, I *must* get an introduction." When I tried to do that, big-mouth Casanova stepped in. You know, I could've introduced myself without his help.
  You may recall, Ms. Autumn, I promised you a letter, and with that, let me formally introduce myself. As mentioned in our initial

Letters to My Lover

introduction, my name is Omari, first, middle, and last. I abandoned my slave name years ago. I come from a talented family of four boys and have the distinct pleasure of being a twin. My brother came out first, so he took most of the talent, along with the good looks. Having a "dual personality" manifested as a twin brother does have its good points, but also a few drawbacks. Being a twin has also endowed me with a part of my brother's "gansta" personality! So please excuse a few of my rough edges. The other side of having "dual personalities" is having dual occupations. I work as a CPA by day and a dancer by night. Yes, I know, it's different.

    I like to keep busy and my current project is the renovation of a turn-of-the-century Victorian mansion. I've been working on it for three years and the house consumes all of my time, energy, and money. (Maybe that's the reason I don't have a girlfriend.) I will confess that the project is a labor of love and personally gratifying. I don't know when it'll be finished because I'm doing most of the work myself. I'm beginning to believe the old phrase, "All work and no play makes Omari a dull boy." (Or in the Great Northwest, a dangerous psychopath!)

    Music and dance have always played a big part in my life. All of my brothers are musicians, and since I never learned to play an instrument, *dancing* is my outlet. I also use dancing to help overcome my shyness, and as you've seen by my clumsy approach, I could use all the help I can get! Dancing's keeps me in good shape and allows me to travel. Unfortunately, with this combination of work, remodeling the house and all the other distractions, I do much less of it now. But dancing's in my blood.

    Forgive me if I seem forward, but your beauty attracts me. So, tell me something about yourself. Where'd you get that beautiful smile? What are some of your likes and dislikes? Do you have any brothers or sisters? How often do you pick up male dancers? Have you ever stuffed any dollars down a man's loincloth? Do you have a boyfriend? (Would you like one?) What types of music, dance, and art do you like? Do you travel? Could I talk you into going out with me sometime?

The First Letters

Let me know if you'd like to come to Seattle for a visit. My house is under construction, but you're welcome. Bring your friends along if you'd like. (*Girl* friends, that is!) When you come, please bring a hammer and hard-hat, we could use the extra help!

If you find the time, please write back, because if you don't, I'll suspect that you only talked to me because of my charm, good looks, witty sense of humor, macho body, and cute butt!

Awaiting your reply,
Omari

Autumn's Reply:

My Dear Omari,
You really surprised me with your letter. I remember you said you'd write, but I never expected your letter so soon. Omari, you have a way with words. I've read your letter several times and each time I extract another tidbit of information about you. I'm letting you know; I've begun a scorecard on you!

I've been telling my friends about your show and of meeting a new friend. Your performance was breathtaking. The combination of music and dance was a sight to see. African music is hot!

Okay, I suspect you're interested in my vital statistics, so let *me* formally introduce *myself*. My full name is Autumn Erica Harper, but call me Autumn. I've just turned thirty and have a younger sister who is somewhat eccentric!

We are adopted. In fact, we aren't biological sisters, but we've always been together. We were in a group home until the age of three and then placed in a permanent home. I know you can tell that I'm of mixed blood. I have some Latin blood and my daddy's Black. An older Jewish couple adopted us. I'll tell you right up front; we live in a unique household. Have I scared you off yet?

I've lived in Portland all of my life and haven't had the opportunity to travel outside the northwest. I'm attending law school full-time and have one year remaining before taking the Bar exam. I

Letters to My Lover

work part-time with a downtown law firm to make ends meet. My current financial situation requires me to save money, so I live with the parents. Are you still there? Well, I guess its confession time.

I'm single, never married and recently getting out of a two-year relationship. I was very much in love, but over time, he expressed his need for more space and eventually left. The relationship took its toll. After that episode, I've decided to be noncommittal and appreciate the single life. Oh, did I mention that he was Jewish. Hey Omari, come back!

You wrote that you have a twin. You mean to tell me there are two of you! So, that explains the split personality "thang." I bet you have him beat on the hip action!

You're creative energy is infectious and I'm happy that we had the chance to talk. Your sense of humor is different, but fascinating. No, Omari, I don't make it a habit to pick up male dancers. However, you looked harmless and I'll confess that your dancing was *very* sexy! Your house sounds like a nice project. I'd love to come up and see it (you) sometime. The next time you visit Portland, we'll go out.

Once again, I found your letter very entertaining, and as promised, here's a letter in return. Writing letters is fun, so let's continue. I hope we meet again soon.

Autumn

Omari's thoughts:

I'm thrilled Autumn wrote back so soon. I knew I stood a chance if I could just get my foot in the door. (And I want inside *that* door!) I didn't want to leave Autumn with the impression I was *too* enthusiastic about receiving her reply, so I waited an entire five minutes before I penned my response.

Now I realize some people don't like my (sick, warped, crude) sense of humor. However, I suspect Autumn's kind of sick herself. So, as they say in the boxing world, "Let's get ready to rumble!"

The First Letters

Letter Two:

Ms. Autumn,
    Sometimes I feel like the luckiest man in the world. Arriving home from another hard day's work, I stop at the mailbox to pick up the bundle of bills. Let's see... the insurance bill, the telephone bill, the light bill, and my psychiatrist bill. There's the doctor bill for the shot I required after dating that "nice girl." (Joke!) Nestled in-between all that bad news is your letter and as soon as I notice it, I get a warm feeling.
    Believe me; I'm pleasantly surprised that you wrote back. So, before I change out of this monkey suit, before I tune into the daily murder report on the evening news. Before I retire to the porcelain library to speed-read the sports section of the paper (a masculine ritual to which I am unfailingly committed), I rip open your letter to see what my newfound friend has to say.
    I read attentively. Your words are like delicious dollops of ice cream, sliding across my palate. I want the moment to linger.
    When I finish, I remark, "She's pretty deep!" But wait, this letter sounds a little suspicious to me. This sounds like her friend "Leroy" has dumped her!
    If that's true, I'm glad Leroy quit you. You're a woman of such class; I know you can do better than Leroy. I ask myself, "Why do you stay with him? He ain't got no money, no job, no class and he ain't even good-looking! What's that broken-down fool got that makes him so special?" My repressed (perverse) personality tries to impose a vulgar thought. Maybe you kept Leroy around because you're hooked on the "big bamboo"! Luckily, the thought didn't register.
    Autumn, I'm glad you wrote back. I couldn't see you writing me off as being another "dawg," after a shot of leg and your bank account. (But can I put those items on my Christmas list?) Another thing, I confess to saying some crazy things at times, but, generally, I'm harmless. (As long as I follow my shrink's advice and take my medication!)
    My dear Autumn, I'm pressed by a busy routine to cut this

Letters to My Lover

letter short. Tonight the crew's in the basement putting up some interior walls. When complete, the basement will be a two-bedroom, Mother-in-law unit. The rent will help me to continue to fund this seemingly never-ending project. Until the next word, please keep those letters coming!

Your (maybe more than just a) friend,
Omari

Autumn's thoughts:
There's something intriguing, but strange about this guy. He definitely thinks "out of the box," but seems relatively harmless. Bizarre sense of humor/terrific body – that's a *dangerous* combination!

I have a girlfriend in Seattle; she's getting married in a few weeks. Maybe I'll ask Omari to be my escort. I need someone who knows the city; also, I don't want to attend my girlfriend's wedding as a single woman. Not that I'm incapable of keeping a man (for longer than a month), but once that champagne buzz kicks in, I want someone around who can handle this tigress.

Maybe I should invite my sister along. You never know; Omari might turn out to be another Ted Bundy! Damn, this is going to be a balancing act because I never know what my crazy sister's going to do. Sis has a flair for the dramatics, depending upon the time of the month! Well, if Omari acts too crazy, I'll just match them up together. Hold on ...that might not be such a good idea. What if they have kids?

Autumn's Reply:

Hello Omari,
Another letter from my newfound friend. Your words of wisdom and crazy jokes are a breath of fresh air. I'm curious: The way you talk, is your daddy a preacher or a used car salesman? I hope you're joking about seeing a psychiatrist. The next time I see you, I might have to lay you down on the couch and see what kind of

The First Letters

craziness is going on in that big head of yours. We'll work out the fee later. (Not that I have any experience seeing a shrink but...uuuhm, oh well.)

I hope you're kidding about requiring treatment for meeting a "nice girl"! Didn't your mom ever warn you about them? I hope you're not going to be so dangerously lusty, but if you are, let me give you some advice; go for the big gals! First, they see limited action and have low mileage. Secondly, they know how to cook! Of course, this advice is for your friends because I might have something else in mind for you. I'll fill in the details in person.

Now let's talk about a few things. We'll start with picking up strange men. (This could include you!) We'll end with "Leroy," and talk about everything in between. Let me tell you a few things about *my* values. First, I never talk to a man who comes strutting up to me as if one leg is six inches shorter than the other one. Second, if his mind's obsessed with his crotch, that's a *strong* indication, we won't have a "thang" to talk about. I don't date "gangstuhs," married men, or substance abusers. Omari, I'm a "working class" kind of woman. What I really want is a BMW, that's right, a **B**lack **M**an **W**orking! As for the "Big Bamboo". Omari, that's free!

Now, on to the next subject, and this might be a little touchy. I suspect by our conversations that you're not looking for some country girl with only one pair of shoes. Being a strong and independent woman means juggling as many balls as possible. It's tough enough without some man (thinking he's going to be in charge) standing on the side, eagerly waiting to throw in another couple of balls for his own self-gratification. Being a strong and independent woman is a delicate balancing act between prospering as an individual and succeeding as a woman. Yes, my career ambitions are important. However, most important is my relationship with The Creator and the desire to have a committed relationship with a lifelong partner. Omari, when I see you again (and I trust it'll be soon), I hope we can sit down and have some serious conversation.

I enjoy reading your letters, yet you reveal little about your deeper feelings. Tell me more about Omari. Do you believe in The

Letters to My Lover

Creator, family, marriage? Would you be comfortable sharing one of your *deepest* secrets with me? I promise to share one with you. (Show me yours and I'll show you mine!) Here are some easy questions: To what type of woman are you attracted? Do you have any intentions of settling down and having a long-term relationship any time soon? Are you presently sleeping with anyone?

I have a friend who's getting married in Seattle in a few weeks. It would be an honor if you'd be my escort. Please look at your calendar for the weekend of March 7th and try to reserve some time for me. I'm going to take you up on the invitation to hang out at your house for the weekend. (You *can* be trusted.) I know you're a busy person, and I promise not to get in the way.

I hope you don't think I'm too forward by asking these personal questions. I want to learn more about you. Please write back soon and let me know if you can squeeze little ole me into your busy schedule. I'll even bring along my hard-hat and tool belt, but only if you let me be the supervisor! I *do* look forward to seeing you again.

Awaiting your response,
Autumn

Omari's Reply:

(Warm, Sweet & Tantalizing) Autumn,
Your letter was very sweet, funny, and heartfelt. (How was it for you?) I suspect you try to portray this determined image of an independent woman. However, when I look beyond that initial impression, it's obvious you're a gentle, nurturing, sensitive individual.

Let me (try to) be serious for a moment and respond to some of your questions. So, you want to know more about the real Omari, huh? Wait a minute; men aren't supposed to reveal their intimate feelings. It's a rare occasion when a man can communicate anything other than, "Give me the remote!" (There I go again. Breathe deeply...)

The First Letters

I'd like to become friends, so I'll be open and honest with you. (Since we're communicating by mail, you can't tell if I have my fingers crossed!) Let me see if I can respond *directly* to your questions.

My first priority in life is giving praise to The Creator and trying to live an honest life. I try to treat everyone with respect and dignity. Believing in marriage, I'm a sucker for intimacy and romance. I'm beginning to feel that it's time to share life's adventures with one *special* person. The big house is being built with marriage and babies in mind. (Perhaps you'd be interested in submitting an application.) In the end, I want to focus my energies on my family.

To your next subject: dating. I hope you believe me when I say I haven't been dating much, *and* I'm a social introvert. Luckily, the dancing gives me a happy balance.

Am I sleeping with anyone? I'll respond by saying I sleep with only one woman, plain and simple. That level of intimacy can be something spiritual. There's no one special in my life now because I'm a work-a-holic. Being alone *does* allow a certain creative space. (It's those split personalities!)

Now, getting to your invitation to be your escort. I joyfully accept! I've been looking for an excuse to see you again. Your invitation moved me towards poetic inspiration:

> I'll have my clothes cleaned just like new
> And dress up, just for you
> We'll show up at the wedding for all to see
> Who knows, maybe someday you'll agree to marry me!

Since we're sharing intimate secrets, let me share one more thing before we go to your friend's wedding. I chew tobacco. Don't worry; they say it tastes sweet when I kiss! Oh, I'm kidding. I spit it out before I kiss!

On the serious side, Ms. Autumn, I look forward to seeing you again. The doors to my dream house (or nightmare) are open. (And so is the roof, it's being repaired.) I *guarantee* you a weekend

Letters to My Lover

you'll remember.

    Let me share another secret. I've dreamed you'd give me the opportunity to pay attention to your needs and pamper you like a Nubian Queen. It's exciting to have met a woman with whom I can share my most intimate thoughts. A woman who makes me feel happy. It's also nice knowing that I've found someone with whom I can exchange saliva! Throw a little champagne into the mix and this could get *dangerous*!

Your not-so-secret admirer,
Omari

Autumn's thoughts:
    I really liked some of Omari's comments. They sounded nice until he went off on the deep end, again. I hope he's taking his medicine.

    I *do* need a place to stay while in Seattle, but I'd better make those alternate plans, just in case. Omari thinks he can shock me by talking crazy in his letters. Well, two can play that game.

Autumn's Reply:

Dearest Mr. Omari,
    You have two distinctive (and schizophrenic) personalities! In one sentence, you're saying these beautiful, insightful things, and in the next, some lunatic starts ranting. Did you take your medicine today? Do you have a friend named Norman Bates? I heard he also lives in a big house!

    You think you can weasel your way out of being my escort just because you chew a little tobacco. Since we're on embarrassing topics, I do have *one* little annoying habit. Passing gas. It's amusing to watch everyone's face as the pungent odor of flatulence slowly creeps across the room, and everyone gets that first good whiff! All the men throw quick glances at each other, trying to figure out who'd do such a disgusting thing! It's all I can do to keep my composure.

    Seriously, Omari, I can think of no one I'd rather have as my

The First Letters

escort to Maylene's wedding than you. Not only will I have a handsome, debonair, and oh-so-suave gentleman, but also the best dance partner in the place. I've really enjoyed your letters and feel that I'm beginning to uncover the *real* you. Omari, you leave me with such a different feeling.

I hope it won't be too much of a problem if my sister Stephanie accompanies me. You said bring women! I should forewarn you; my sister "beats to a different drum." It might be a good idea to have some of your medication available, *just in case* she has one of her infamous outbursts of madness! For her, you might want to have that available in double doses! Do you have any eccentric friends? She's looking for a date. I wait with anticipation to see you.

Your charmed friend,
Autumn

Chapter Four
The Wedding

Omari's thoughts:
    I hadn't suspected the bride-to-be was Caucasian. Haven't I filled my quota of Afro-phobic White folks for the month? Maybe I'm a little too sensitive about being around large crowds of White's, but why is it that all of the men comb over those few strands of hair? Why did everyone keep handing me his or her coats and car keys? Not that I didn't mind the tips, but I came to drink champagne and party!
    Autumn was looking good. I suspect Autumn's sister, Stephanie has been working at the glue factory a little too long. Adding insult to injury, the girl's also butt ugly! That's a dangerous combination! Lucky for me, brothers stick together. I told Lloyd I had a special lady coming into town this weekend and I needed him to run some interference for me. He quickly agreed. You see, Lloyd's a "dawg".

Letters to My Lover

He'll try to hump any leg! The girl could be bug-eyed and toothless, one or both legs missing, eight-to-eighty, blind, crippled, and crazy; Lloyd's not partial. He'll still try to make a play for the booty.

However, Autumn's sister was *truly* exceptional. Lloyd telephoned me in the middle of the night, ranting like a lunatic. "You should've heard that damn, crazy-ass woman babbling and speaking in tongues. She tried to call the devil-direct!" Lloyd was so rattled that he stormed out of his *own* house and ended up sleeping in his car. Sister Stephanie must be out there!

Autumn's comments:

I'll never forget this weekend. Omari was a true gentleman. He went out of his way to me feel like a Queen. To be honest, girlfriend hasn't been treated like that in a long time. I have to admit, this guy might be worth keeping. He even took me sightseeing in his friend's Ferrari. I didn't think he knew anyone at the wedding.

Omari's house is big, but he has lots of work to do on that thing. I could see the stars while lying in the bed (but there were no skylights). Searching three different bathrooms, to find one with running water was an adventure! I'll admit; it was fun to get out of Portland for the weekend and do something different. I wish Stephanie hadn't acted so damn stupid. Omari might think it runs in the family!

Omari's Letter Following the Wedding:

Ms. Autumn,

You looked stunningly beautiful at the wedding, better than the bride. You should've warned me in advance that Maylene was wealthy. You know I'm a man of great ideas but little cash! The food was great! But, why did everyone think that I was the waiter?

Our dinner conversation was a real turn-on. I find your independent thinking very attractive. Did you notice that foul odor at the dinner table? I suspect your sister was passing gas! You did try to give me the low-down, but I think Sis has one foot in the "Funny Farm" and the other on a slippery bar of soap!

The Wedding

Seriously, I hope you enjoyed stepping away from the wedding for a moment and letting me show you that fantastic view of the city. How often do you get to ride in a Ferrari? Nice, huh? Maybe I should feel guilty, but how could I resist when some person I don't know hands me the keys to his luxury sports car, along with a crisp twenty-dollar bill, and asks me to park it. Hope he didn't notice that I took the long route. I surely hope he won't notice the little dent I put in the fender while trying to double-park in the handicap zone!

Now, let's talk about your beautiful brown skin and the way it complemented your dress. If I close my eyes, I can still smell the delicate fragrance of your hair.

Being in an atmosphere of love made it a very special evening. The way you pampered me made me feel like a King. We danced so smoothly and you were the center of my universe. It was as if only our world existed. To hold you in my arms felt special. Being your escort was a dream come true.

It was nice to have you around for the weekend. I hope the accommodations weren't too Spartan for your taste. Rarely do I receive such sophisticated ladies (or any ladies at all). Usually, they look at the house and say, "Excuse me, but did you notice there's no roof on this house? I ain't staying here cuz something might come in the middle of the night and bite me!"

Autumn, I'll be honest with you. I woke up in the middle of the night, and the thought crossed my mind to tap on your door, just to make sure everything was all right. But the moment I stepped out of bed, the phone rang. It was Lloyd ranting something about your sister speaking in tongues and it killed the moment!

Again, thank you for a beautiful weekend. I'm intoxicated by the memories of our time together.

Yours truly (and more by the minute),
Omari

Letters to My Lover

Autumn's Letter Regarding the Wedding:

Omari,

Never in my life have I had such a memorable time. Omari, you're such a suave and debonair escort. You treated me like a Queen. When I close my eyes, I'm in your arms and we're dancing. What a sensation. When I first saw you on stage, your dancing was so strong and masculine. Your gentle touch and self-confidence displayed your tender side. I like that in a man. However, I do have one question. Was that a pencil in your pocket, or were you just happy to see me?

Our stimulating conversation, the dancing and spending time with you made the weekend special. You were the focus of my world. Of course, you know I want more. Staying the weekend in your house was quite an adventure. I've never slept in a house with half a roof. It rains a lot in Seattle, so you'd better fix that soon!

I'll confess, after attending the wedding and having such a stimulating time, the idea crept into my mind to tap on *your* door in the wee hours. Unfortunately, after eating so much rich food, I was somewhat bloated. If I'd gotten excited and let something funky hit the air, you might have suspected it was me passing gas at the dinner table! Whoever it was, I'm sure she's extremely sorry for not being able to stand up to the pressure!

Thanks for a wonderful weekend.

Autumn

Omari's comments:

After reading Autumn's letter, my alter ego was beginning to mess with me. Something's telling me not to let her get too close, but I'm not listening. Besides, my other head is beginning to stir. "Big Fella" wants a piece of the action! There's a war going on between the head that handles self-preservation and the head that needs to handle preservation-of-the-species. Maybe I'd better insert a little pause into this emerging romance and cool off a little. But, my question is, how could Autumn confuse "The Big Fella" with a pencil!

Chapter Five
Bumping Heads

Okay, I'll confess to "stretching the truth" a little. I wasn't dateless before meeting Autumn. I did date. However, when you have "rehabber's disease," also known as "Lack-of-funds-itis," women don't stay around too long! One evening, a couple of women surprised me by coming over unannounced (a single man's greatest fear). I'd casually dated both for over a year, but it was their first time meeting. To make a long story short, there are two slots open in my social calendar.

Let's look at this philosophically. Although Norma was a psychopath, she'd have me hollering for sweet Jesus in the middle of the night. That I'll always miss! Lucia could burn some serious bacon and loved to keep me fat and happy! Oh, the woes of a single man! Maybe now is the time to give Autumn "The Treatment". She's far enough away that we won't bump heads.

Let me also clarify something, because I don't want you accusing me of something that I'm not, such as untrustworthy, a liar, a fast-talking "player," or even a "Stank Ho!" My relationships with women are unique because there is something to appreciate in everyone; it's just a matter of discovery. Realizing this uniqueness in an individual doesn't mean you want the entire package. Let's use cars as an example. I walk through the dealership and see a car with a beautiful body style; I appreciate its curves. I see another car and appreciate the power of the engine. Yet, another has a beautiful paint job. Nevertheless, they're three distinct models. There's no need to own all three cars; it's better to utilize them as various needs arise. Not that I equate women to fast cars, but I realize different models fit different occasions and one size, unlike condoms, doesn't fit all. I'll admit to having a little "dawg" come out in me occasionally, but that's human nature.

Right now, I have to get some work completed on this house. This remodel project has taught me that a cold bed, with nobody in it but you, speaks volumes about your personality!

Chapter Six
The Big House

Let me tell you a little more about "the big house". It was a follow-on project, preceded by three other fixer-up houses. Remodeling was a hobby of mine. I loved finding older homes and restoring them to their former glory. I'd live in them until the next project came along. Then, I'd rent the house to a young family willing to exchange a little "sweat equity" for reduced rent. Providing affordable housing was something I believed in. After doing this a few times, I thought I was ready to venture into the higher end of the marketplace. Boy, did I dive into the deep end of the pool!

The big house project began over dinner with my dear friend Leo. We were talking about the obstacles associated with the project, when Leo starts drawing on a napkin. He was describing how to lift a house that had fallen off its foundation. I was reluctant, but he convinced me to concentrate on the business portion of the deal and let him accomplish the engineering side. Little did I realize the magnitude of the decisions we made that evening.

The negotiations to purchase the house began at one hundred thousand dollars. In the end, I picked it up for fifty thousand. That may sound like a bargain, but the land was worth fifty thousand dollars, and the house was worth nothing. To knock the house down and haul it away would cost fifty thousand; hence, that became the rationale for my offering price. Two weeks after the negotiations began; I was the proud owner of another headache.

The house *was* falling apart, but I'm drawn to its grandeur. It was an old Victorian, built in 1905 and standing on an acre of land, which included a beautiful view of Lake Washington. We knew it needed to be stripped down to its "bones" and rebuilt. When I told my friends about the purchase, they were excited. However, when they saw the place, they thought we were crazy! No one could stretch their imagination enough to envision the house as Leo and I saw it.

It's amazing to look in retrospect at some of the things that stick in our minds. I remember my boss being so jealous because I

The Big House

purchased another house. It riled him that a young, enthusiastic, Black man was utilizing multiple dimensions of his mind, trying to get ahead. I was also a person who wasn't going to be denied. Today, I'm the boss and he's the worker, but that's another story.

Soon, Leo and I began the task of lifting the house and replacing the foundation. That's when I realized my mistake in letting Leo talk me into buying this house.

Leo influenced me and I have the honor of calling Leo my best friend. I could trust Leo with my life, but not with money. Yet, no matter what, we realized our human bond, and between us, there were no secrets. Leo knew all my limitations and weaknesses, and I knew his. Together, we were strong and indivisible. I was just crazy for letting him talk me into this project!

It took a while, but we started gearing up the project. Purchasing the biggest timbers we could find and placing them underneath the house, we began the lifting process. The place looked like a construction site. Early in the lifting phase, we realized we couldn't raise the house with the fireplace attached, so we removed it, brick by brick. That took three days. Next, we disconnected the plumbing, then the electricity. Finally, after repeated attempts to lift this monster, it broke loose from the foundation.

We used 50-ton jacks at thirty different structural points for lifting, and inch-by-inch, the house began to rise. It creaked and groaned, as it started the assent. Lifting this house was dangerous and we paid for every mistake in blood. However, after six weeks, the house stood eight feet off the ground, and we had all our fingers!

Sleeping in the house at night, you could feel it sway and hear it moan; telling us of its pain. When the wind blew, the entire house shook, as if experiencing an earthquake. We worked hard and fast to pour a new foundation. Next, came the process of lowering the house. After four months of the most dangerous work ever attempted in our lives, the house was on its new foundation. The hard part was over. (We thought.)

The house looked like a war zone. Every wall was cracked and plaster dust covered everything. Yet, we'd pulled off something

Letters to My Lover

unbelievable. We had jacked up a house, poured a new foundation, and set the house back down. To our amazement, no one was killed!
Now are you beginning to understand why I'm single?

Omari's Letter:

Autumn,
My "mind's eye" pictures our time together at the wedding. The joy on your face and the smell of your essence still linger in my mind.
Autumn, what's the definition of a gentleman? A man who gets out of the shower to pee! All right, I won't act stupid (easier said than done)!
Lora is putting together a six-week tour that will take us to Europe. The combination of death-defying work, and no playtime has put me in a funk, so I've decided to go. By the time you receive this letter, we'll be in Europe.
When I return, let's go on a long weekend. We could visit some friends in the San Juan Islands. A recurring dream is to cater to your every desire. Would you like to make the dream a reality?

Omari

Chapter Seven
On the Road to Europe

Boarding the airplane to begin our European adventure, it feels as if some divine force is coming along with us. Good omens begin as soon as we sit down. I introduce myself to the distinguished-looking man sitting beside me, "Hello, my name is Omari." He turns and replies, "Hello, my name is Dick Gregory, a pleasure to meet you." The first leg of our trip, from Seattle to New York, is memorable. Mr. Gregory and I have one of the most heartwarming, stimulating conversations I can remember in years.

On the Road to Europe

Seven of us go on the tour - three women and four men. As we board the Boeing 747 that will take us from New York to Belgium, Lora leans over and whispers to me, "Is it my imagination, or are we the only Black people on this airplane?" I look around and reply, "Look on the bright side; this means no one will be sitting beside us!" Unfortunately, the airplane is full and it's difficult to sleep in a seat designed for a person half your size. Furthermore, the seating proximity makes you intimately aware of your neighbor's personal hygiene. Of course, the well-endowed German looking woman sitting beside me not only claims the armrest as her personal space, but insists on taking off her shoes! (Then, I see her eyeing my airplane peanuts)

Changing nine time zones in less than a day reminds me of a game we played when we were young. The bigger boys would grab the little guys and spin us around until we could barely stand! I felt that way as I struggle with the crying baby behind me, along with the woman beside me. She's lifted the armrest, which allows more of her rotund rear-end to encroach upon my personal space!

"Flight attendants, please prepare the cabin for arrival." The captain's words signal our landing. My body feels as if it's gone ten rounds with Muhammad Ali and lost a lopsided decision. It was twilight when we left the States and morning when we arrived in Belgium. Lora points to Tendi's slobber-stained chin and laughs. "At least he got a little sleep; that's more than I can say." Our crumpled clothes and sleepy eyes paint a surreal picture of humans stepping out of a sardine can as we disembark.

Lora is the first to notice the man standing at the gate with a sign reading, "African Dance Troupe". "Hey, mister, I think you want those people over there." Little Casanova points to a group of older Germans, who are dying to get off the plane and fire up that first cigarette. Everyone starts laughing!

We're in luck because this tour provides a bus and driver. The bus has all the comforts of home, making traveling much easier. After our all-night flight, we want nothing more than sleep. The driver assures us that our reservations were complete and we were going directly to the hotel. We're all so sleepy that it takes an effort to insert

Letters to My Lover

the keys and open the doors. Lora's last comment as the doors shut behind us is, "Get some sleep because we're dancing in twelve hours!"

Morning

"Good morning, heartache. You old gloomy sight. Good morning, heartache. Thought we said goodbye last night." Billie Holiday sings on the clock radio. I begin to wake from a restful sleep. Laying there for a few minutes, I look up at the ceiling, trying to regain my senses. "Might as well get used to you hanging around. Good morning heartache. Sit down." Her sultry voice sings so eloquently.

Stretching my arms, I prepare to get out of bed. When my feet hit the coolness of the tile floor, I realize that we're in Brussels. My eyes begin to focus and I look around the room to see the guys still sleeping. "Great! This'll give me the luxury of taking a long, hot shower and allow my muscles to unwind from the trip."

"Good morning, heartache," I sing. The hot water hits the back of my neck, smoothing out the kinks. "I'm glad you can dance better than you can sing. Shut up, so I can go back to sleep," Little Casanova's grumpy voice says from the other room. "Wake up you guys," I shout from the shower. "I've got an idea!"

Wrapping a towel around my waist, I walk back into the sleeping quarters and open the curtains, just enough to let in a little light. Taking off my towel, I begin snapping everyone's ass. "Leave me alone and shut that damn curtain," Tendi demands from beneath the covers. "Wake up, you guys. I've got an idea that's gonna make us some money!" I knew the word "money" would capture their attention, and it did. Everyone's head pops out from beneath the covers. Shielding half-shut eyes from the light and still fighting sleep, they slowly sit up in bed and listen to what I have to say. I take the time to look in everyone's sleepy eyes and begin to explain...

The Money

I describe a little scheme to put some cash in our pockets. It takes about thirty minutes to get the guys up and another thirty to get organized. Making sure not to disturb the ladies sleeping next door,

On the Road to Europe

we leave our room and stroll down the hall toward the hotel lobby. Picture us: four handsome brothers "posing" at the top of a staircase. We're dressed in all black—black hats, black sunglasses, black sleeveless shirts, black pants, black leather gloves, and military boots! Man, you could've heard a pin drop in that lobby. We descend the stairs, one slow step at a time. Knowing that every eye in the place is on us, I break out in a big laugh and remark, "This is gonna be like shooting fish in a barrel!"

Carrying our conga drums, we make our way toward the City Square and Marketplace. The centerpiece of the square is a majestic stone church built in 1205. It towers five stories high with a cathedral tower, holding the bells, which chime so beautifully, marking the hour. It's three o'clock in the afternoon. In the middle of the square stands a beautiful marble water fountain; skilled artisans must have worked for generations to build it. The outer rim of the square is ringed with the booths of farmers selling their goods. The entire square is paved with a smooth stone, making it easy for the people to maneuver their carts.

Being the only black people in town, we draw a little bit of attention. It makes us feel special. (Is this our fifteen minutes of fame?) With everyone watching us, we decide to give a show (in return for some money, of course). The grand entryway of the church is the perfect place to set up and execute our ten-minute performance.

We set up our conga drums and begin to play. Immediately everyone turns around to explore this curiosity. We blow our whistles to a Brazilian rhythm, signaling the beginning of our performance.

Little Casanova always starts our dancing. We use him to attract the crowd. He knows all the newest hip-hop steps and is an accomplished tap-dancer, as well as an African dancer. He reminds me of an updated version of Sammy Davis, Jr. His facial expressions capture everyone's attention. This guy can *really* dance *and* make you laugh! That's how he got in good with the girls. But, the bottom line is, his talent. He's unafraid to compete with the "big boys". Finishing with a triple spin, and landing on one knee, Little Casanova is a tough act to follow.

Letters to My Lover

Shelton dances next; he shows off his athleticism. Shelton's sheer physical prowess impresses everyone. His solo act includes gigantic leaps performed to the rhythm of the drums. He repeatedly leaps the height of a person's body, making these primal faces as he freezes in motion. There's a certain attraction in watching men dance together and Shelton makes everyone stop what they're doing to watch. He uses his power to push everything to another level. We let Shelton dance as long as he wants, because his stamina has no end. Shelton's finale is a series of impressive back flips, taking him across the stage. I'm there to catch him as he finishes his flips. Walking him offstage is my cue for entry. By his time, the entire square is watching. The crowd cheers Shelton as he exits the stage. He takes a bow, still flexing his muscles.

I begin my routine by jumping up onto my hands and moving to the rhythm of the beat. Clapping my feet like hands and using my hands like feet, I continue to dance for minutes on end. The crowd grows more appreciative the longer I continue to dance on my hands. Finally, I flip back to my feet and take a bow.

We draw in the crowd by getting them to clap. Tendi goes into his act on the conga drums. Tendi makes the drums talk, as he interacts with the audience. We invite people in the crowd to come and dance. A few couples step forward and oblige.

We begin to blow our whistles and make our way back to center stage with a fancy boot dance. Slapping our boots, we add another layer of rhythm into the mix. This choreographed, precision stepping is urban and nothing these folks have witnessed before. We finish our performance with a series of high kicks and freeze, as the conga drums stop with split precision.

Standing to take our initial bow, the crowd gives us a thunderous round of applause. We take off our hats and bow. This is the signal for Little Casanova to get out there and act cute. He begins to solicit money from the crowd. For all of Little Casanova's character flaws, he's good at getting people to donate to our cause. Like a true artist, he works this crowd. Finally, it gets to the point where so many people are clamoring to donate; we must all go out and get the money.

On the Road to Europe

We're keenly aware of the unwritten rule regarding street performance. After ten minutes, you clear out in a hurry! Any longer, and you're likely to have the cops breathing down your neck, shaking you down. The problem is that you can't solicit money without a permit! Of course, if you give half the money to the "Policeman's Fund," they're less likely to cite you and take it all! We quickly pack our congas and prepare to go. Little Casanova collects the remainder of the money. With our pockets full, we walk briskly across the square toward the hotel, as inconspicuously as possible. (Right!)

Back in the hotel, we count our new made fortune. Two hundred dollars for ten minutes' work. Not bad! The feeling is sweet because we know Lora's gonna make us practice anyway. Now we can tell her we're finished and ready to go for tonight's performance. Needless to say, we will *practice* in every city of the tour.

Germany

Creativity is an element that has a mind of its own. It comes and goes at its own discretion. The power of creativity really hit us when we played in Frankfurt, Germany; it took us on a magical journey.

You can sense the excitement and anticipation in the air the evening we start our thirty-minute set. Intimate settings are nice because they enable you to mold the atmosphere, like shaping a piece of clay. I've also grown to appreciate short sets, (at my age, they cut down on the need to carry oxygen)!

African music has a universal element within it that touches every soul. On this night, the strength of the music is undeniable, and the energy infects everyone in the crowd. Within our performances, we make no distinction between the audience and the performers. Additionally, we use the energy generated from the crowd for our inspiration. As we hit our first notes, you could feel the excitement.

Halfway through the first song, I jump off the stage and grab everyone wiggling in their seats, getting them up to dance. It's as if the crowd is looking for an excuse to join the party and grabbing them provides the spark. Spontaneously, the place explodes into a celebration of song and dance and inhibitions fly away. A young brother

Letters to My Lover

jump's onto the stage, grabs the microphone, and starts rapping to the African beat. The place goes wild!

Soon our celebration draws the attention of the local restaurant and sports bar. People start coming from all directions to witness our music and dance. A couple of other brother's jump upon the stage and begin playing the conga drums. This pushes the music to a fever pitch; my ear even picks up someone in the audience playing a coke bottle! The music is rocking and the energy has picked up a life of its own! I signal my fellow dancers to jump down into the audience with me. We break into a choreographed dance, not missing a beat. Watching these women move their asses to this energetic beat is a remarkable sight! As the crowd swells, they open into a circle to give us room to dance. The women begin to dance flirtatiously with everyone. Next, we form a dancing line and take our music into the streets.

We play one song for forty minutes and the crowd has swelled to hundreds. After forty minutes, I can no longer go on. Every ounce of energy in my body is gone.

Creativity man, what a special feeling. It happened in Frankfort, Germany. Creativity tapped us on the shoulder, sang a sweet song in our ears, and took us all on a magical journey!

Paris

A contingent of people greet us when we arrive in Paris. I love France because people greet you with a kiss. French people are open-minded, yet nationalistic. If you don't speak the language, they give you this condescending attitude. We give an appropriate response by singing a South African greeting song. The harmonies are so beautiful that everyone can't help but put aside our cultural differences and embrace the moment. From then on, things go from good to better. Little did we know, but we're representing the U.S. State Department on this particular gig. We knew something was up when we arrive at a five-star hotel. The view of the city is breathtaking!

Our first performance is for a governmental affairs function. It's a high-level, multicultural event, with members of the United Nations

On the Road to Europe

in the audience. Our performance is superb. Even those stiff diplomats are tapping their feet.

For weeks, I'd been working on a solo dance piece entitled, "Goodbye, My Friend." The idea originated as a healing gesture regarding the recent loss of a loved one. I ask the group if I could premier the piece after intermission. Everyone thinks it's a great idea.

Years of dancing have made my body tight and for this dance, I oil my body and wear only a thong. Just before the music starts, a feeling I've never experienced enters my body. I step upon the stage, realizing that dancing is the reason for me being able to travel the world. Dancing is allowing me to touch a special place within people's hearts. Here I am, dancing in front of some of the most powerful people in the world, yet I have them right in the palm of my hand. My chest stands high and I feel like a lion.

I select Gato Barbieri's piece entitled, "Don't Cry, Rochelle." His sax expresses so much passion that it inspires me. That night, in some strange, poetic sense, I can feel every note. I *am* the music and the stage becomes my playground.

Jazz is about elegance and the music allows me to express a full range of emotions. Feeling long and lean, I crawl to center stage. Placing my palms flat on the floor, I begin a slow ascension onto my hands. Like a circus performer, I make every muscle in my body rip and flex. Slowly, elevating my feet, I balance on my hands. The music makes me do these things and I can only follow. The audience responds with applause, as I balance myself on one arm.

Tumbling back to my feet, I race across the stage and kick high into the sky. It feels as if I can defy gravity. Turning in midair and landing in a split. The music sounds so sexy that I begin to move on the floor, as if making love. Making soft and sensual moves, I surrender to the feeling. Gato finishes his serenade and the stage lights fade with the music...

After our performance, people introduce themselves, remarking how my dance touched something special within them. One person in the crowd makes it a point to search me out and compliment our show. Marcel is the French diplomat assigned to the UN. Our

Letters to My Lover

conversation quickly becomes more than mere small talk. Expressing my desire to see as much of Paris as I can in three days, Marcel obliges by personally offering his services. To reciprocate, I promise to go into the schools and teach a few dance classes.

The next three days are a blur of non-stop activity. We visit the art museums, the Eiffel Tower, and the best restaurants. Marcel also provides a diplomatic identity, affording us special treatment.

While demonstrating a dance at school, a teacher catches my eye. Playfully, I bring her in front of the class to show the kids how to dance with a partner. Her name is Martinique. Obliging my request, she extends her hand to be guided through the crowd. The kids laugh as we elegantly dance to the music. Martinique plays along, as if part of the show.

After class, I ask her to be my escort for dinner and a jazz club that evening. Martinique enthusiastically acknowledges my request by answering yes, in five different languages.

Marcel arranges for the group to have dinner at one of the most elegant restaurant in Paris. Martinique arrives looking like a model straight out of Vogue magazine. The combination of her style, sophistication, and sensuality make for a wonderful evening.

Lora, dressed in African splendor, is a Queen and projects nothing less. I can tell that Marcel is enjoying all of the trappings of his influence and the wine flows liberally. After the third bottle, I feel *so* French!

After dinner, Marcel asks the limousine driver to take Martinique and I on a tour of the clubs and to ensure our safe return to the hotel. He gives me an approving wink and nod. I open the limousine door for Martinique. This is no ordinary woman. She's warm and charming, full of laughter and vitality. Martinique displays so many of the traits that I desire in a woman. She also brings out the gentleman in me.

Our night turns out to be one I'll never forget. The dinner, the music, and meeting new friends leave me sitting on top of the world. The limousine pulls up in front of Martinique's house at 3:00 a.m. Our embrace feels so genuine that I didn't want to let go. I deposit a kiss

On the Road to Europe

on her sweet lips. "Promise me that you'll attend our show tomorrow afternoon." Martinique speaks softly. "Omari, I wouldn't miss it for the world."

Our final show is a good one. The energy is high and we really work the crowd. Martinique shows up and is looking as beautiful as the night before. During the second set, Lora asks me to perform the solo piece again. However, this time, I present it as if dancing privately for Martinique. I can tell she appreciates it. After the show, she approaches me and delivers a passionate French kiss! (Down, boy!)

After the performance, we continue our sightseeing, with Martinique as my private tour guide. She makes it a point to hold me close.

Marcel ensures Martinique's attendance at dinner that evening. Her beauty and sophistication continue to intrigue me. Martinique speaks to me in English, and without missing a beat, turns her head, and speaks French with Marcel.

After dinner, Martinique and I go back to the hotel for a nightcap. I light a few candles to create an ambiance of love within the room. Martinique kisses the back of my neck and whispers, "Can I spend the night with you?" Now, how can a "brotha" resist an offer like that!

We begin our mating dance and can't get enough of one another! We make love, get up, and take a bath, only to begin making love again. I remember our sweet embrace as we stand on the balcony watching the sunrise. It was so romantic that I didn't want it to end.

I have a feeling that Marcel will be a friend for many years to come. As for Martinique, she introduced me to a sophistication and elegance I've never experienced before. She brought out the fire within my soul and I have no regrets about our time together. I realize one thing; I'll never forget Paris or Martinique!

Italy

Italy was special for me because I arranged to have granddad come over and join us. Granddad was celebrating his 89th birthday

Letters to My Lover

and I wanted to give him a special gift. Granddad was an excellent tap dancer and I wanted him to witness the talents that he'd passed to his daughter, who is my mother, and on to me.

The people in Italy are beautiful and the women held a particular fascination. Their deep, dark looks and sexy demeanor are irresistible. By the time we arrive in Italy, we've grown fond of getting attention from intriguing women. Yet, Italian women held a special spice. Italian women love to flirt, hug, and kiss, which are three of my four favorite things I like to do with women. During the days, we go to the beach to hustle up some money with our street performance. Afterward, we hangout in our swimsuits, picking up the women we wanted to "entertain" for the evening.

On the second night of our engagement, we again find the magic. Tendi plays like a madman and we dance as if performing for the Gods. Lora casts her spell upon everyone and we begin improvising. Somewhere within the dance, my spirit ascends into heaven.

It's great having Granddad in the audience. I can see that our dancing affects him, because he begins walking around without his cane, something he hasn't done in years.

Omari's thoughts about the European tour:

Have you ever experienced the feeling of knowing that all of your energy forces are aligned and working as one? Traveling to Europe and doing something I love so much gave my creativity a chance to explode. Seeing different countries and having them as our personal playground has changed my view of the world. Dancing for six weeks put me in the best shape of my life. Realizing this artistry gave me a first-class ticket to see the world, *is* a revelation!

During this tour, I met some of the most influential and beautiful people in the world. It's as if dancing formed a bridge and gave me a particular style and grace. Dancing gave me the opportunity to shape my emotions into a beautiful art form. Dancing gave me elegance and an air of sophistication. Dancing gave me the ability to speak to anyone.

On the Road to Europe

Dancing gave me wings and I soared like an eagle! Yes, from this trip I've come to realize, "Dancing is my mistress and I will *always* love her."

Okay, I'll admit it; I'm a "dawg!" Do I feel guilty? No, because I'm a "dawg." Well, maybe a little bit. Only because I know that you're reading my thoughts and questioning my morality. If it weren't for that, I'd feel differently. Of course, I'll never tell Autumn what really transpired in Europe. Sometimes discretion is the better part of valor.

I remember reading a poem written by Nadine Stair, age eighty-five and she said; "If I had my life to live over again, I'd climb more mountains and cross more rivers. I'd take more chances and succeed by accident. I'd have more real problems and less imagined ones."

My experiences allow me to realize you only go around once in life, so why not live it to its fullest. Yes, I feel a little guilty because I like Autumn. Maybe I should start my next letter to Autumn like this...

Dear Autumn,

You'd never speak to me again if you knew of all the mischief we got into.

Omari's Letter:

Ms. Autumn,

Back in the States and back to reality. However, I'm back with a new attitude. One thing is for sure, I don't want to see a glass of wine.

The house was still standing when I got back. Nobody burned it down. (Although, I did leave specific instructions.) It's also nice to sleep in my own bed (under a completed roof).

The past six weeks have been like living in a surreal dream. I hope I didn't offend you by leaving so quickly; yes, I'm impulsive. Autumn, going over to Europe was an experience of a lifetime. There are a few things that I want to share with you. (Including some saliva!) Here's another secret, I miss you and want to see you soon.

Letters to My Lover

    I hope you've been thinking about our get-away. We're taking my friends boat up to the Orcas Islands. Ya wanna come?

Omari

Omari's thoughts:
    Okay, I was trying to plant a seed in her mind. (In addition to other places!) I wanted to see Autumn again because Europe taught me that it's good to have your oil changed on a regular basis. I've come to realize being a gentleman will only get you so far and letting the "dawg" out occasionally keeps everybody happy. (Especially the "dawg"!)
    Paris re-ignited my senses and Autumn is the perfect candidate to help me fan the flames of passion. So, "Come on baby light my fire!"

Chapter Eight
The Maintenance Man

Autumn's thoughts:
    Finally, Omari is becoming interested. I bet something happened in Seattle. Maybe a few of his women friends met the competition. Maybe he went over to Europe and had a hot little fling. A woman can sense those subtle changes happening within men. You can look in their eyes and see the guilt, or in a "dawg's" case, the bravado. Men sometimes act like "dawgs" and it's just a matter of time until they're caught humping the wrong leg.
    I was beginning to worry that Omari was taking his gentleman act a little too far, or didn't consider me attractive. It's important that men understand and act upon a woman's desire for passion.
    I remember when I'd feel guilty because my man wasn't touching me, but I don't feel guilty any more. My guilt went away when I found out that my man had a little "something on the side," which was why he wasn't taking care of business on the home front.

The Maintenance Man

My guilt turned into anger when I realized that he was out there getting his at my expense. That was a year ago. Now it's a completely different story.

You know, perception and reality can be two different things, and my feet are firmly planted in reality. Since Omari's living in Seattle and I'm in Portland, I feel no guilt about having someone local. That's where Donavon (who Omari affectionately refers to as "Leroy") enters the picture. He's my local "Maintenance man".

I met him after my last relationship. Donavon isn't the sharpest brother on the block, but he's built the way I like em. (Although, I do wish the brother had a little more common sense.) Donavon's good for one thing, which is a once-a-week "appointment". Our arrangement worked beautifully for the first three months; then the real Donavon showed up. That's when I found out the brother didn't work and thought his once-a-week *privilege* allowed him access to my personal property. I don't think so! Yet, Donavon was good in bed! Eventually, our sexual liaison began leaving me with an empty feeling. I wanted more than unemotional sex. I wanted to feel. When I expressed my desires regarding communication and commitment, I received excuses instead of reassurance. That's when it became clear; it was time to move on. Unfortunately, there were times when I'd find myself wanting to backslide and succumb to the desires of the flesh. Hence, Donavon a.k.a. Leroy likes to call from time to time to see if I've changed my mind. Lately, I've been changing my mind. Now don't get me wrong, it's been real good sexually, but this is a dead end street and I'd be fooling myself if I didn't admit it's time for a change.

The deciding moment to end our liaison came when Donavon and I were having sex. I realized that he was only thinking of himself because he didn't even look at me, or I at him. That's what it was sex, nothing but sex. (I wanted to ask him if he was having as much trouble thinking of someone else as I was!)

Omari was gone a long time and I miss talking with him! Believe it or not, I missed his (sick) sense of humor. The last time Donavon phoned, I was hoping it was Omari calling from overseas to say hello.

Letters to My Lover

I'm glad he made it back safely. He sent me a postcard from every country, but I missed reading his letters. You know, it's time for me to shift gears. It's time to change mechanics and let someone else "fine tune" this Jaguar. You just relax, Omari; it's time you let this woman sit in the driver's seat! (Excuse me sir; will you please look under the hood and check my oil?)

Autumn's Reply:

Omari,
    Your invitation to go on a boating excursion is tempting. I hope my stomach's up to the challenge. After spending time with you at the wedding, I've been looking forward to seeing you again. You must know that I'm envious of your ability to make things happen and get out of town. When will my time come?
    Omari, you're on official notice: I'm interested in you (if you don't realize that already). Now, I don't consider myself the possessive type, but the idea of sharing what I like is not an option, especially when it comes in a handsome, debonair, suave package like you.
    Thanks for the postcards from Europe. Maybe when we're on the island, you'll tell me some of the things you did. Europe sounds exciting. I'd love the opportunity to explore another culture. If you really want some excitement, invite me on the next trip. I promise, you won't be disappointed!
    How's the house coming? I know you said the opening in your roof is a big skylight, but I didn't fall off the turnip truck yesterday.
    Count me in on the boat trip. I look forward to spending some quality time with you and your friends.

Autumn

Chapter Nine
The Boat Trip

My friend Al was proud of his boat and he should be. He found a vintage 1935, 38-foot, wooden-hull boat and completely refurbished it. The boat sat wasting away in dry dock for five years before Al bought it. After the purchase, the boat was out of the water another two, undergoing a complete restoration. He would work on it every weekend. In fact, it was his home away from home. When the boat was ready for the water, it was completely upgraded.

The boat was outfitted with a lavish interior and able to sleep four people comfortably. The paint job was a testament to Al's meticulous attention to detail. The boat was beautiful and we completed a two-week shakedown to ensure that it was once again a seaworthy vessel.

A week later, Al and I are stowing equipment in preparation for our trip to Orcas Island. After all the equipment's been properly stowed and secured, the ladies drive up to the marina.

"Ahoy there, mates!" Autumn shouts. She sees our final flurry of activity in preparation for shoving off. We embrace and exchange a few kisses. We haven't seen one other since the wedding and it feels good to hold her in my arms. (I hope she doesn't ask about Europe!) "Hi Al, my name's Autumn. Let me introduce you to my sister, Stephanie." Autumn grabs Stephanie and positions her in front of Al, allowing him to inspect "the goods". "A pleasure to meet you both," Al answers. I notice his response to meeting our traveling companions. I can tell he feels that he's getting the short end of the stick. (And he is!)

I owe Al this one. I wanted to get even for the blind date from hell he set me up with about a year ago. The lady turned out to be pro-wrestling fanatic with an affinity for country music. Rarely do you find a Black woman who has the entire Garth Brooks collection and can sing every song.

Letters to My Lover

Al's a down-home type of brother who's been divorced for a couple of years. He didn't have any trouble meeting women, but in the years after his divorce, he's come to understand the difference between quantity and quality (and about to get a refresher course). We've been friends for a decade or so and both of us are notorious for pulling practical jokes. For us, it's always open season for a good laugh. After having worked on the boat for so long, it's easy frame Stephanie as the poster child who'd help him with an oil change. He's very proud of completing his project and it's only appropriate that we christen the maiden voyage by breaking in the boats beautiful interior in a "manly fashion".

"Portland's three hours away, but we were beginning to wonder what was taking you guys so long." I grab Autumn's hand to steady her, as she boards the boat. "We left early, but stopped to get some breakfast. Hope you guys didn't mind." Al, still trying to be a gentleman, interjects, "Your timing's perfect, so let's shove off and begin our weekend."

"Bow rope released," I shout and head towards the back of the boat to release the last remaining rope holding us to shore. "Stern rope released." I jump on board and we're off.

Al's charted the waters and mapped a course leading us out of the inlet and into the mouth of the Puget Sound. We'll be traveling on the water for about six hours to get to Orcas Island. One strip of water in the Strait of Juan de Fuca is unprotected by the shore and will demand special attention. The extra effort we've taken to ensure that everything is secure will be tested in those waters.

We cruise by houses built along the shore and gaze in amazement at the beauty and peacefulness of the surroundings. "The water's smooth while we're in the bay, but it might get a little choppy when we hit the open water. Let's run through the safety procedures to make sure everyone understands them. With only four of us on the boat, it's best to give everyone a little task to spread out the work and make the trip fun." He emphasizes, "If anyone feels queasy, make sure you go outside and breathe some fresh air. Make sure you stick your head out the window if you feel you're gonna puke." (Spending

The Boat Trip

six hours smelling what someone else has upchucked isn't a pleasant sensation. Not to mention what it would do to Al's beautiful interior work!)

Al and Stephanie strike up a pleasant conversation as Al shows her how to handle the wheel. Standing behind her, he reaches around and put his hands on hers. "It looks like they've settled in pretty good," Autumn remarks. We climb out on the deck to catch the midday sun. It's been two months since the wedding and Autumn looks beautiful. "I wonder how long it's going to take before Al finds out Stephanie speaks in tongues," I whisper. She elbows me in annoyance. "That's not a nice thing to say." Knowing all the time, she's thinking the same thing. "Sorry."

We cruise along the mouth of Puget Sound and enter the ten miles of open water. It looks like things are going to get a little choppy. When the waves begin splashing us, we retreat into the comforts of the cabin. Al takes command of the boat and points us toward a bearing that will get us across the straits quickly. I stay with Al at the wheel while the ladies retreat into the bow of the boat. The boat is beginning to rock with a steady motion. "Let's give a little bit more throttle to get across this open water faster. It's getting a little rough out here," Al says. You can see the tides crossing in the water ahead of us. The next mile is going to be exciting. Al calls down into the cabin and asks the ladies to make sure everything is secure. I go outside to ensure that everything is tied down. Shutting the door to come back into the pilothouse, I notice that there is no sound coming from the cabin below. I go to check on the ladies and, opening the door, I see two people pale as ghosts.

They both look like they were ready to liberate their breakfast. "Are you guys all right?" Already knowing the answer to that stupid question. "You guys need some fresh air! Let's go up to the pilot house and open a window." I grab Autumn's hand to steady her, but she's already in trouble. "Maybe we should hurry!" I get Autumn into the pilothouse and lower a window. "Breathe deeply and look out towards the horizon; it'll help you feel better." Al has a little smile on his face. He tries to reassure Autumn that it's normal to feel a little

Letters to My Lover

seasick. This *is* her first time crossing Puget Sound. Al's been on the water long enough to understand the do's and don'ts of boating. One "don't" is eating eggs before boarding a boat.

I go below to see if Stephanie is in any better shape. Unfortunately, she's already in the process of liberating her breakfast. I say *unfortunately* because she's neglected to prepare herself for the inevitable. At the last moment, she grabs the nearest container, which happens to be Al's prized cowboy hat and deposits her breakfast! I know there's gonna be hell to pay later on, but the highest priority is to get Stephanie into some fresh air. I grab a sick bag and exchange it for the overflowing hat. Grabbing Stephanie by the back of her waist, I push her toward the upper deck, trying to steady her as the boat continues to rock. She bends over and blaaaaaaaaa... The sick bag goes one way and her breakfast goes another. "Oh shit – all over Al's new leather coat. Come on Stephanie, let's get upstairs!" Now I'm pushing her up the steps, trying to get her head out the window before Al sees what's happening! Blaaaaaaaaaa.... He knows what's happening now! Stephanie pukes on his pants leg! Blaaaaaaaaaaa.... "What the hell, hey baby get your head out the window!" Al isn't smiling anymore! Blaaaaaaaaaa.... On that attempt, she gets half of it out the window and the other half on the seat below. Autumn pulls her head out of the other window to see what all of the commotion is about. Watching her sister getting sick triggers her own motion sickness, and the next thing we hear is Blaaaaaaaaaaa.... Al and I listen in stereo as the two sisters try to outdo each other. Blaaaaaaaaaa... Blaaaaaaaaaa... Blaaaaa!

It takes another four hours to reach our destination. We feel sorry for the ladies; because once you've started getting seasick on a rocking boat, it isn't easy to get un-sick. You think you're through, once you've liberated the contents of your stomach. That's when the dry heaves start and you begin puking up your toenails!

The boat now looks and smells like a floating latrine. The decks outside the windows are stained with cheese omelets. The seagulls add insult to injury by stopping by for a little breakfast and deposit a load of shit on Stephanie's head, which remains stuck out

The Boat Trip

the window. We feel sorry for both of them, because all we see for the remainder of the trip are two big asses contracting and releasing. They continue to sing that familiar song, Blaaaaaaa…! By the time we get to shore, I bet a couple of people are going to have to perform an "underwear check"! Blaaaaaaaaaa....

By this time, Al's one "pissed" brother! Any notion of a romantic weekend getaway is replaced by the thought of having to clean up behind a stranger, who's ruined the interior of his boat! Additionally, when you're watching your date throw up for hours on end, the last thing entering your mind is a good, saliva-exchanging kiss! But, after Al saw the condition of his hat and coat, he couldn't have gotten a hard-on even if Stephanie would have gotten butt naked and greased up with Crisco right in front of him!

When our friends arrive to pick us up, their first comment is, "What's that funky smell?" It's early evening and there isn't enough daylight left to begin the task of cleaning up. By this time, <u>everyone</u> wants off the boat. Needless to say, there'll be no exchange of sex this evening!

The next day, we return to the boat and begin swabbing the decks. The paint job is permanently stained with a color known as "Puke"! The smell reminds me of the time I walked into the bathroom after big "Bubba" had been on a three-day taco-eating binge! It's bad! The weather isn't cooperating with us either, so we collectively decide to cut short our mini-vacation.

The return ride is just as adventuresome as the ride up, because the ladies know what's in store. So, Al and I have the distinct pleasure of sailing back across Puget Sound with two ladies having their heads stuck out the windows, singing that familiar song, Blaaaaaa...! The birds show up again and used Stephanie's head as target practice! Let's just say, this will be a weekend we'll remember!

Letters to My Lover

Autumn's letter:

Omari,
      I write to say that it was wonderful to see you again. However, due to the circumstances that evolved, if that's the way you make me feel, I never want to see you again! (Joke) I know my intestines are clean, because I felt some of those heave's come from way down under! I've never been so sick in my life! Everyone was looking at us on the way back to Portland. Our heads were stuck out the window for the entire trip. The first thing my sister did when she got home was to cut off all her hair. Bird shit is some powerful stuff! She's also sorry for ruining the interior of Al's boat. I hope he can get that smell out of there. He didn't think it was very funny when my sister offered to give him her beat-up hat in exchange for ruining his.
      I thought when you meet someone; you put your best foot forward. Let's put it this way Omari; it can only get better, because you've seen me at my worse. If there's one positive thing about the weekend, Al never got the chance to hear my sister speak in tongues. (Although, he was making up a language of his own!)
      Omari let me make amends for our last encounter. I'm sure we can do better. I'd like to invite you to come visit me in Portland. We have some wonderful rose gardens around the city. Let's pack a picnic basket and hang out. There's a nice river walk (but you're going to have to walk on the river side). We also have a few places that play culture music. We can dance the night away.
      So, how about it? Would you like to come down for a visit? You see, Omari, I'd like nothing more than to get you away from all your distractions and help you relax. Will you please pencil me into your calendar?

Autumn
PS. For your information, we burned our clothes!

Chapter Ten
The First Trip to Portland

Autumn,
    Hmmmm, a weekend in Portland sounds heavenly. You always come up with good ideas. Of course, you know that the idea of a weekend with you brings many things to mind. I'll keep most of those thoughts to myself. You're inked-in Autumn; in two weeks, I'm yours for the taking. I wait in great anticipation to see your pretty face.

Omari
P.S. Al hasn't spoken to me yet!

Omari's comments:
    I knew I was making progress when she invited me to visit her stomping grounds. Autumn's living with her parents, so how's this going to work? Does this mean I have to be on good behavior? How am I going to get any loving at night when I'm stuck sleeping in the guest room? Maybe I should offer to stay in a hotel. (But the ones I frequent charge by the hour.)
    I hope her sister's not around. If she is, I hope she speaks in a language I can understand. I hope her mom didn't teach that poor child everything she knows. I hope I can get a three thousand-mile oil change.

Autumn's Reply:

Omari,
    I'm glad I could entice you to get away from the house for the weekend. Of course, there's some ground rules to be established before you come. First, you must come with a relaxed attitude. A friend of mine is out of town and I'm housesitting, so we have our own place to stay. Next, you are in my town and at <u>my</u> mercy for the entire

Letters to My Lover

weekend. Therefore, our dream about having a picnic among the roses will become reality.

My parents are going to want to meet you, but I must warn you, if you think my sister is somewhat eccentric, so are my parents. If my mom starts talking your ear off, please excuse yourself and go to the bathroom. That's about the only place you'll find silence. You're going to have to stay in there a while because she'll be standing beside the door waiting for you to come out. I suggest taking the sports section in with you. Next, if my dad starts talking about his investments and wants you to look at them, tell him you don't have any money and run in the other direction as fast as you can. Finally, if my sister comes up to you and starts talking to you in a strange language, watch out, because you've just entered the Twilight Zone.

Now, if I can ask a personal favor of you. I want you to forget about your work and the construction going on at the house for the weekend. Come down here and give me your undivided attention and I'll give you mine. Let's try to create a weekend like we did at the wedding, where only we existed. (I promise not to puke on you.) You see, dreams *can* come true and we have the ability to turn ours into reality. Omari, I'm moist with anticipation regarding your arrival.

Autumn

Autumn's thoughts:

I knew I was making progress when he agreed to come down to Portland. Should I tell him how eccentric my parents *really* are? I hope my sister takes her medicine. Maybe I should slip a dose or two into her marijuana brownies. Once Mom starts talking, Omari's going to know where my sister got all her smarts. Boy, it's going to be hard for Omari to be on good behavior for an entire weekend. Maybe I should slip him a dose or two of my sister's medicine. Maybe this isn't such a good idea. This could be the making of a good movie. Maybe I should call Spike Lee.

The First Trip to Portland

Things to do before the weekend:
> Remember my Sister's medicine.
> Remember my Mother's medicine.
> Inform Father that Omari has no money!
> Call Donavon and tell him I'm out of town for the weekend!
> Change the sheets!

After the Portland Visit:

Autumn,

    Autumn, I confess to having a wonderful weekend. Our time together is etched in a special place within my heart. Your presence was heavenly and allowed me to discover new dimensions of you. This weekend has given me a newfound respect for you. (And what you have to go through with your family.)

    To share and express love with you was intoxicating. Autumn, you're a breath of fresh air and I feel so alive. Thank you for being a special friend.

Omari
P.S. Thank you for not puking on me.

<u>Omari's thoughts:</u>
    Sometimes the things I write are so full of shit! First and foremost, I got my oil changed. (That's a load off my mind, if ya know what I mean.) Secondly, I know where her sister got her mental illness. Oops, I mean her creativity. However, I'll be nice and say her parents are somewhat eccentric. Third, we had a nice time and Autumn's turning into a true friend. This weekend, she got a little piece of my heart. Maybe it's time to quit acting so silly and show her some of my redeeming qualities. Bow-Wow!

Letters to My Lover

Autumn's Letter:

Omari,

I'm glad we were able to create our own little dream world, if only for the weekend. Omari, I must confess, the more I'm with you, the more I want from you.

I felt comfortable as we explored each other, yet vulnerable as you peeled away the layers of my resistance. It's been a long time since I've been with someone who made me feel like a woman. I knew I was in good hands.

I'm sure it was obvious by the look in my eyes that I wanted you. It was a difficult balancing act trying to find out more about you. Yet, the more I discovered, the more I wanted and after a beautiful evening, I was committed to loving you.

Omari, I was swept away by your attention. When you looked deep into my eyes and kissed me ever so slowly, my heart skipped a beat. Your gentleness and confidence of being in charge left me wanting for more. Your attention to my desires encouraged me and I melted, as you explored all parts of my body. I felt wanted. Later in the night, I was pleasantly surprised to be awaken by your sweet caress, yet forceful manner. Waking up in the morning and feeling your firmness had me burning with desire. As I reminisce about our weekend, I feel my body tingle with excitement.

My parents just love you. In fact, Mom's asking if you have any single brothers. I think she's still trying to pawn off my sister on some poor unsuspecting soul. (She might be looking for a little something on the side herself.)

While you were preparing to leave, thoughts raced through my head. Our weekend felt too good to be true. Omari, I look forward to being in your arms again. I feel so lucky to have shared your company.

Autumn

The First Trip to Portland

Autumn's thoughts:

Wow, what a nice weekend *and* I got my "3000-mile checkup!" Omari's a nice guy and it felt nice being treated like a woman instead of a sex object. I was able to relax this weekend, and by the time Omari left, I know he felt no tension. To be honest, he turned this alley cat into a little kitten.

Omari's comments:

I purposely put a little time between our letters. After putting another notch on my belt, my "big head," regained some control over the "Big Fella". Please don't get me wrong, Autumn's a wonderful woman. But, after I threw that thousand-pound gorilla off my back, I'm beginning to think clear again. Getting a letter from Autumn is still a special gift. I just needed reassurance that she wants me for more than just my body. (Right!)

I could also see a change in her attitude and after reading her last letter, the word *commitment* kept entering my mind. Now my homeboys always told me to respect the word *commitment* and I do. When I look at some of my married partners, the word *commitment* is like the baton beating the crap out of Rodney King. *Commitment*, yes dear anything you say, POW! But, it's tough to put a chain on this "dawg"!

Chapter Eleven
The Big House – Free Rent

It was fun playing out this vignette with Autumn, but this house project was demanding my attention.

The house was now 3700 square feet and growing fast. Due to its condition, coupled with the amount of work yet to be completed, Leo and I decided to exchange free rent for work. Over the years, Seattle housing had become so expensive that it was difficult to find

Letters to My Lover

decent, affordable housing. The house wasn't decent, but *free* is affordable, so utilizing the barter system seemed like a good idea.

Use of the word *free* brings another dimension into any equation. To think that you can get something for nothing brings out the derelict in all of us. When our *free rent* advertisement started running in *The Seattle Times*, a parade of people wanting something for nothing came knocking on the door — people in every condition that life could spit out. Personalities like Jason, from the movie *Halloween,* made cameo appearances. The place became an off-Broadway theater production, with me as the stage manager. Some of the characters are noteworthy. Let me describe a few of them. There was:

Will: Dumb as a brick, but strong as a horse. If there was something dusty, dirty, hot, stinky, or just downright nasty, we'd send Will to do it. He knew where he stood in the pecking order of things.

Larry: A redneck who was out of step with the rest of the world. Alcohol was the root of his problem.

Brain Dead: This guy had been on drugs for so long, he was brain dead. He'd go around the house talking to himself. The scary part was that he'd also answer.

Jay: A "rock star." Every available dollar Jay earned went to smoking crack. Jay would tell you anything to get you to support his habit.

The Thief: We caught him stealing from the rest of the people in the house. We nailed him into his room and forced him into slave labor until he paid back what he stole. He tied a bunch of sheets together and jumped out of a three-story window, escaping with only the clothes on his back. We never heard from him again.

The Biker: Stopped through for a few weeks to let his ass heal, then hit the road again.

The Dike: Yuck!

Enrique: A good worker, but he drank every night. His other unusual trait was that he watched TV all of his spare time, all of it! One day, the cops arrived and arrested him. We never heard from Enrique again.

The Big House - Free Rent

Eric and Brian: Two hustlers who'd steal the diamond ring off their dead grandmother's finger, at her wake. They'd hustle credit cards from lonely women and always had a steady stream of willing customers.

Harvey: He was an electrician who marched to a different beat. Harvey had a drinking problem and his wife threw him out of the house. One cold winter night, he came staggering home and went into his room. He came out telling everyone, there was a rat in his bed. We thought he was telling another one of his drunken stories! We went up to his room and Harvey was right, there *was* a rat in his bed!

David: An electrician recently released from prison. That was his obsession. His problems also stemmed from alcohol. One night after a drinking binge, he drove his car into Lake Washington.

Courtney: If anyone had ever sold her soul to the devil, it was Courtney. She was a habitual liar who'd lost the capacity to think of anyone other than herself. She represented greed in its purest form.

Warren: This gentleman was saving up his money to marry his sweetheart. Warren always put in his time and did excellent work. It's easy to respect someone whose word is good. A year later, Warren sent us an invitation to his wedding.

Ken: A framer who bragged more than he worked. If you caught a fish two feet long, Ken had caught one three feet.

Many more troubled characters made cameo appearances at the big house. They say necessity is the mother of invention, but the adventures associated with this house went far beyond that. These adventures enabled me to look at life from a completely different angle. (Like the underside of a toilet bowl.) Yet, the house was a dream, even though it seemed like a nightmare at times. The free rent part of the project was my "character building" phase. Being a stage manager to this cast of characters wasn't fun, but it sure was exciting!

Letters to My Lover

Chapter Twelve
Letters Later...

Omari,
    Thoughts of you are dancing through my head and I feel compelled to write them down to help arrange them. How's my handsome friend? I've been thinking about you lately and feel somewhat frightened and embarrassed to confess something, but I will anyway.
    Omari, for the first time in my life, I've actually allowed myself to desire something so definite that it scares me. I desire to be close to you, to touch you. I want to feel you physically and emotionally. I want to share my soul with you. To express these emotions makes me feel vulnerable, but the joy of the experience outshines the potential for being hurt. (Except for stepping on that rusty nail in your house!) I don't want to scare you away, but I'm falling in love with you.
Autumn

Autumn's thoughts:
    I gave Donavon his walking papers! That "Bend over babe, Big Daddy's coming home" was getting old. He'd always pull out that stupid stopwatch just before we'd begin making love. You'd think he was running a hundred-yard dash. To be perfectly honest, I'm due for a change.
    Come aboard Omari, cuz I'm ready for romance. I'm ready for the ocean of love to sweep me away, only to be rescued, and given mouth-to-mouth resuscitation (with a little tongue thrown in for flavor). Take me, Omari, I'm yours!

Omari's comments:
    Hey man, reading her last letter scared, yet excited me. She's openly talking about commitment. What's she been smoking!
    The funny part about the whole situation is I'm volunteering to walk into this open mine shaft. That's what love will do to you. It'll

Letters Later...

cold-cock you upside your head with a baseball bat. All the while, you're thinking that you're under control. Like the boxer that's been knocked out and when he comes to, he asks his corner, "Did I get him?"

Our visits are becoming frequent. Autumn's officially blocking the rest of "the trade".

Omari's Reply:

Autumn,

Your letter was quite insightful and strange as it may seem, you know me very well. There are moments when I'm strong and determined, yet unsure of it all.

Do you know what I want Autumn? I want to wake up in the morning and feel you next to me. I want to smell your fragrance and feel your body heat. I want to look underneath the covers and see your beautiful body. I want to make love early in the morning, only to fall asleep in your arms. I want you to tell me all of your secrets, knowing they're safe with me. I want to lick your body, watching your expressions as you succumb to the pleasures of my desires. I want you, Autumn.

Omari

Omari's comments:

Now, you know if a brotha's writing some shit like that, the girl has his nose wide open! I've stepped on a land mine and don't realize that I've died and gone to hell for all of my womanizing sins! I've been pick pocketed of my manhood and don't know its missing! I'm so far gone; even my "dawgs" can't bring me back to my senses. So, just knock me in the head, steal my money, and take my shoes. Someone call the mental hospital and tell them to bring their little white wagon, because this boy's sick!

Our weekend excursions are becoming frequent. Autumn comes up to see me one weekend, and the next, I visit her. Her

Letters to My Lover

parents let me stay at the house and even ignore my tipping into her room at 1:00 in the morning. At breakfast, Autumn's mom asks her why she's praying in the middle of the night. (Yes! Sweet Jesus, here I cum Lord, here I cum!) She expected these outbursts from Stephanie, especially when she didn't take her medicine, but now it's happening to Autumn.

Autumn's Reply:

Omari,
    Thoughts of you continue to swirl within my head. I've come up with a list of things I love about you:

Your smile
Your laugh
Your intellect
Your perception of reality
Your logic
Your practicality
Your resourcefulness
Your strong hands
Your gentle touch
Your dark eyes
Your soft skin
Your embrace
Your compassion for your friends
Your graceful movements
Your energy
Your thirst for knowledge
Your love of music and dance
Your sensitivity
Your respect for others
Your conceptual capacity
Your openness
Your generosity

Letters Later

Your passion

These are just some of the things that I love about you (not to mention the pencil in your pocket), but I think you get the idea.

Autumn

Chapter Thirteen
The One-Year Anniversary

Omari's comments:

This is a milestone for me. I've been dating the same woman for a year. This must be love! Usually, when a woman finally discovers my "charming personality," she quits calling and changes her phone number.

The other women have moved on to other "dawgs". I was naive enough to tell them about Autumn, the girl of my dreams. Talking about leaving faster than the last cold beer at a Texas barbecue!

Autumn and I are seeing each other on a regular basis. Not only does she have a dresser drawer in my room, she also has her own closet. I say this with a sense of bachelor reluctance in my voice, but we're happy.

I've become so pathetic; I've given my "dawgs" all the phone numbers crossed out in my little black book. I even went as far as changing the beneficiary on my life insurance policy from Mom to Autumn! Finally, I knew things were changing when I placed a picture of Autumn on my desk at work. The sexy accountant on the fifth floor quit coming by to say hello after that stupid act.

My friends began noticing the feminine touches around the house. Gone are the posters of big-breasted women that covered the cracks in the walls. They've been replaced by cute poetic sayings meant to inspire. (Hell, those big-breasted women were doing pretty good in the inspiration department!)

Letters to My Lover

I feel like a reformed alcoholic, who, after so many years, kicks his habit. (Or the soon-to-be crack-head, who takes his first hit and realizes, "This is what I've been looking for my entire life!") Whatever it is, I've got it bad! Somebody please shoot me in the head and burn the carcass before I infect the entire "dawg" population!

Lora and I are still dancing and our act is in such high demand that we double our prices and no one even blinks. The band performs some weekends without me. I'm down in Portland getting my "fix". When I show up for dance practice, Lora gives me a look that says, "You better watch out, you're spending too much time with that girl, she's going to get you." Of course, she's worried that my distraction is going to eat into our creative time.

The house is making significant progress. I'm beginning to think that buying this thing wasn't the biggest mistake made in my life. I didn't like devoting every spare minute of time to five different projects, nevertheless the feeling of being broke. Yet, I'm beginning to realize that if we stay the course, one day, we'll look back and only remember the good times. Damn, I wish that day would come!

In retrospect, it's evident that meeting Autumn was the best thing that happened to me in the last year. (Although fixing the hole in the roof ran a close second.)

Autumn's comments:
Omari and I have known each other for a year. To be honest, I love being treated like a Nubian Queen.

In my previous relationships, the personality disorders started showing up around the third month. Then I was concerned about changing phone numbers and the locks on the doors.

Donavon's gone, although he calls occasionally when he gets drunk, trying to make a booty call. That "dawg" has died. The other men also quit calling; it's as if "dawgs" can smell another's territory. (I always wondered why Omari would go outside and pee on my mom's bushes. Although it was helping them grow.)

The year has passed quickly. I'm admitting to my friends that I have a boyfriend. I feel so in love, if I had any credit limits left on my

The One-Year Anniversary

cards, I would have given it to Omari, for his house project. Hey ladies, I knew he was mine when he volunteered some closet space. I even convinced him to get a cell phone, so I can contact him on demand! Omari is so hooked; I could've asked him to wash my dirty drawers! (Excuse me honey, but you've missed a spot!) Can I get a high-five ladies!

Autumn's Letter:

Omari,

Your letters are the highlight of my week. I go to the mailbox everyday in anticipation of hearing from you. My girlfriends want to know if you have any friends. They think your friends must be like you. I hate to say it Omari, but some of your friends are nothing more than sex-crazed "dawgs". Wait a minute, that's a perfect description of my friends. Maybe we ought to throw a party and let your "dawgs," meet some of my "felines". Throw in some cheap wine and I'll bet you someone's leg will get humped by the end of the night!

Omari, I don't know why I act so silly around you, but it seems to be so natural.

Autumn

Chapter Fourteen
The Big House – When Does a Dream Become an Obsession?

Over the past year, the house has gone through a major transformation. There were times where the obstacles felt overwhelming, yet, "necessity is the mother of invention." I remember my friends' faces when they'd come by to check on our progress. (Along with my mental state.) At first, they'd ask, "Are your crazy?" Gradually, everyone saw things coming along; they'd offer their own ideas. They were amazed to witness a house coming back to life.

I'd suggest the same thing to everyone who came around. "Come over on Saturday and donate a day of labor." To my amazement, some would show up and pitch in. Yet, the question remained, "When does a dream become an obsession?" I knew there were times when I crossed the line and became one of the "free rent" characters.

The previous winter had been particularly nasty. An arctic cold front came through Seattle and stayed for a few weeks. We set up a wood stove for heat and burned the sections of the house we were demolishing. Because of the many air leaks in the house, the stove burned constantly. Finally, it got so cold that all the pipes, as well as the water in the toilet froze.

Everyone left to seek shelter elsewhere. This turned out to be a blessing in disguise, because I was tired of dealing with all the social misfits. Mother Nature gave me an excuse to clean house.

Unfortunately, by the end of the cold streak, every pipe in the house had broken. The Creator works in mysterious ways, because when the insurance claims adjuster knocked on the door and saw our dilemma, he immediately wrote a check large enough to outfit the entire house with new plumbing. We used the money to replace the plumbing, the electrical wiring, and the heating system.

Even so, that winter *was* a traumatic experience. I'll never forget having to use the bathroom wearing a coat, hat, gloves, and still

The Big House - When Does a Dream Become an Obsession?

having my butt freeze to the toilet seat! (Excuse me, but do you have any warm water on you?)

By spring, we'd replaced every window in the house, doubling the size of the lake-facing windows to exploit the view. We then moved into the basement to begin reconfiguring the first and second floors. During this phase, everything in the house was covered with plaster dust. Leo and I were designing the rooms as we went along; slowly, the house began to make the transformation into its new configuration.

Leo incorporated some of the big beams that we had used to lift the house into the new design. This gave it an open-space configuration. The bricks from the chimney were laid into sculptured sidewalks, with fish patterns within the design. We planted trees to stabilize the hill and created paths to traverse the hillside. Leo's artistry was amazing. By the end of spring, he had planted 15 varieties of fruit and nut trees on the property.

However, in the back of my mind the question remained. "When does a dream become an obsession?"

Chapter Fifteen
Come Dance with Me

We have a dance engagement in Victoria, Canada. We're performing at the Governor General's mansion. Will you accompany us?

Omari

Letters to My Lover

Chapter Sixteen
Georgia on my Mind

Omari's comments:
A colleague called unexpectedly to offer me a lucrative assignment in Atlanta, Georgia. He was providing outlandish incentives for me to accept it.

To be honest, I *was* growing weary of living in the Northwest. The years of hard work were beginning to take their toll on me. I felt tired. Having the sun shine only two months out of the year didn't help the situation. The opportunity to relocate to Atlanta sounds appealing and I'm listening.

Telling Autumn about my newfound opportunity is a different matter. The worse thing a confirmed bachelor can do is to begin thinking beyond his "Big Fella," which is what I'm doing. I'm considering Autumn's feelings and how relocating to the other side of the country will affect our relationship. Should I think about dropping my bachelor title? (I hear the boxing referee picking up the count, "four, five, and six"... and I hear my corner man shouting, "Get up champ! Get up!")

Autumn's Letter:

Omari,
I'm excited about the Canadian getaway. I've never told you, but to watch you dance is an emotional experience. Your ability to express yourself is an inspiration from The Creator. To watch you being swept away by your emotions touch's a special place deep inside of me.

Autumn

Chapter Seventeen
Canadian Getaway

To get to Victoria, Canada you must drive your car onto a big ferry and cross the Puget Sound. It's a beautiful day and I'm hoping this boat trip doesn't bring back memories of our last escapade on the water. The sun and the ocean air feel refreshing.

The band is standing at the front of the boat when Little Casanova shouts, "Look you guys, a whale!" There it is, a killer whale, swimming alongside the ferry, snorting water from its blowhole. A few minutes later, a bald eagle swoops down on the water, grabbing a salmon in its talons. Being so close to nature and holding Autumn in my arms feels heavenly. The contrast of her warmth against the coolness of the ocean air awakens my senses. The two-hour ride to Victoria is relaxing and I begin to unwind.

A Magical Night

Our first performance in Victoria is a private show. A full set of workers greet us as we drive up to this beautiful seaside estate.

In a show of Canadian hospitality, we're treated to dinner. We dine in a formal dining chamber set up to accommodate the fifty guests. The china looks like artwork and a full complement of utensils accommodate every serving. The ceilings are thirty feet high and elaborate carvings accent the full-length windows, facing the harbor. Everything about this place reeks of money.

We begin dinner with Dungeness crab. The next entree is smoked salmon, then lobster. It's going to be hard to dance! Autumn is savoring every moment of this fairy-tale. As a gesture to acknowledge her beautiful presence, I reach under the table and squeeze her hand. She squeezes back, letting me know her appreciation for being invited.

The owner of the estate and host for this affair is an older woman who takes a particular fancy to Autumn. She quickly discerns that we are in love. I compliment her beautiful place; she acknowledges

Letters to My Lover

the compliment by giving us a tour of the estate. I relate the story of building the big house in Seattle, yet, surrounded by such opulence is a humbling experience.

To repay such generosity, we want to give a fine performance. Lora, in her infinite wisdom, looks around and begins to sing an African welcome song. Her voice sings out like an angel. We join in on the next chorus, creating harmonies that are the perfect complement to such a beautiful setting. When we finish, Lora begins to recite a story passed down through the generations of her family. Lora pulls us into her story, casting a spell over everyone in the room. Then she begins to dance. After Lora finishes, Tendi burst into a conga drum solo. The drums sound full in the cathedral-like setting. Soon, the music flows through me and I can't resist. I execute a series of back flips, which transport me across the room. Lora sings out an African chant and Lora begins to dance with me. She looks in my eyes, then over at Autumn. Lora wants me to present the dance to Autumn.

She laughs, knowing the effect my dancing will have. Racing across the floor, I go into a headlong slide, ending at Autumn's feet. I begin dancing before her. Imagine my surprise when she begins rubbing my body and licking her fingers. She's tempting me to take her! I grab Autumn by the waist and lift her above my head. Sliding her down my sweaty body, our dancing becomes foreplay. Autumn and I dance out our seduction, as our guests watch in fascination.

Back at the guest-house, after the set, Autumn and I shower together. That evening, she throws away all her inhibitions and lets out her wild side. We climax together as the harbor clock strikes twelve. Afterward, we laugh, feeling so alive and knowing this moment will remain etched in our minds for the rest of our lives! Our night in Victoria is magical and sets the stage for the rest of the weekend.

Feeling Autumn's warmth, as she sleeps next to me is heavenly. I recall a joke in which a bachelor is asked, "What is the definition of eternity?" The bachelor retorts, "Eternity is the time in-between, when I cum and she leaves!"

Now, I didn't feel like a bachelor. I love the intimate feeling of holding Autumn and watching her sleep in my arms.

Canadian Getaway

The Next Day

"Good morning." I kiss Autumn's forehead, watching her wake up. "Omari!" She snuggles next to me.

We sit in silence at breakfast, still absorbing the events of the night before. "I realize why you guys get so much work, Omari. Your performance last night swept me into another world." Autumn sips her orange juice.

The noonday sun feels good. We take a barefoot stroll on the beach. The waves crash into the rocks offshore. The brisk sea breeze makes our eyes water. I grasp Autumn's hand. "Autumn, I have some good news. A colleague is offering me an assignment in Atlanta. He feels that I'd be the perfect candidate. I'm listening to his offer and trying to understand what he wants to accomplish. Of course, I'm excited that my colleague thought of me for this particular assignment. However, I'm torn by the effect this might have upon us. I'll be honest with you; the offer intrigues me. But, I want to talk with you and get your opinion. Two heads can be better than one in these situations."

My words stop Autumn dead in her tracks. She takes a deep breath and slowly exhales. Another wave crashes into the rocks. "Wow, I don't know what to say." She takes another deep breath. I squeeze her hand, just to make sure she's all right. She doesn't squeeze back. I turn and look to see that glazed-over look of a boxer, trying to recover from a clean shot to the head.

That evening, we have the honor of dancing for the Governor of British Columbia. Our show is superb. Autumn however, is displaying a stark contrast from the previous evening. Though appreciative, she sits quiet and reserved. I watch her anxiously throughout our performance. She gives me a pensive smile, trying to pretend that everything is all right, yet her face tells a different story. She's been thrown a wicked curve ball.

The ferry ride home takes forever. Lora asks, "What did you say to that girl?" That's when I tell Lora about my job offer. "Good for you," Lora replies. Yet, Lora can make the best of any situation. "This'll give us another place to play in the future. Lora puts a funny

Letters to My Lover

expression on her face. "That's why the little princess has such a long face. She thinks she might be losing her prince. Sometimes women are reluctant to give up a good thing, even when we know it might lead to a better tomorrow. So, you go brother-man, because the lion needs lots of room to roam." I feel relieved. Lora helps me clarify my thinking. Presenting such a bitter pill to Autumn is another challenge.

We watch Seattle grow larger in the distance. Soon our weekend journey will end. Struggling to organize her thoughts, Autumn asks if we can go outside and get some fresh air.

"Thanks for a wonderful weekend. It's been so beautiful being part of your world." She takes a deep breath. "What an action-packed weekend. All of this activity has my head in a spin. Of course, you can see that I'm stunned by your news. However, I've made it a point to look at the positive side of things. I've always felt very strong as an individual, but your news sent reality crashing down on me. Listening to you speak about your newfound opportunity, I was excited. Now, I'm speaking as a woman when I say that your words about opportunity translate into the reality that you're leaving. I have a sinking feeling deep down inside my stomach and I can do nothing but dwell in the misery of the moment. The feeling still reverberates in my head, as I think about the most painful aspects of what you've said. It keeps translating into that painful pit in my stomach. I know this is a good thing for you. Unfortunately, I can't help but look at it from my own selfish perspective. Like the weather, there's been a cloud cast above me. Even though our weekend isn't over, I eagerly anticipate spending more time with you. I want to talk about our future."

Autumn gives me a strained smile. I see her need to be reassured that everything will work out. "Can I get a hug, baby doll?" Our long embrace takes us into the port of Seattle.

Wow, what a weekend!

<u>Autumn's comments:</u>

In my heart, I knew Omari was too talented to stay in one place for too long. It'd be selfish and shortsighted to think that I can keep him here if he wants to go. This man's going to do what he wants. Maybe it's best to encourage him and hope for the best. I've met plenty of men in my life and most of them have turned out to be forgettable, but not Omari. He makes me feel alive. I do know that I've fallen in love and don't want to lose him.

Chapter Eighteen
A Seattle Perspective

Living in Seattle was easy. Jobs were in abundance because of companies like Boeing and Microsoft. According to the material possessions, I've acquired most of the trappings of success.

Seattle brought many cultures together and there was the harmony among the races. You could date anyone and no one cared. But this openness brought a dilution within the Black community, because the community wasn't large enough to sustain itself.

I'd listen to my brothers extol the virtues of diversity, knowing that it came at the expense of our sisters. I watched many of my brothers acquire a taste for white women, while neglecting our sisters. This disassembly of Black culture was a bitter pill to swallow. Yes, I confess to dating outside my race. Let's just say that the taste of the "forbidden fruit" is enticing. I also know my origins and will never forget who bore me into this world. A Black woman.

A generation of Blacks in Seattle had married outside their race and moved to the suburbs to escape their confused identities. Their kids grew up with an aversion to other Black kids who lived in the "Central Area". I had uneasily witnessed this assimilation of Black culture.

The more I thought about it, the more I realized that it *was* time to leave Seattle and move on to the next adventure. The assignment would act as a catalyst for change.

I remember Granddad telling me, "Son, you can't discover new oceans unless you have the courage to lose sight of the shore." Now, I understood his words.

Letters to My Lover

Omari's Letter

Autumn,

I've sorted out things in my mind and decided to accept the assignment in Atlanta. We're close to finalizing the details. Sometimes I'm baffled to see how The Creator works, but I understand how important it is to be patient. Something is driving me toward this change.

The move will be a chance to expand our relationship into new directions. Yes, our lives are changing, but for the better. Let me reassure you that you're the highest priority in my life and I won't do anything to endanger our relationship. I hope you're with me on this.

Omari

Autumn's Reply

Omari,

Watching you dance took me places that I've never been before. Spending time with you on the ocean was wonderful and I loved our walk on the beach. The feeling of having your warm arms wrapped around me was heavenly.

In spite of my stunned reaction to your news, I'm happy for you. All my negative thoughts about you leaving are disappearing.

Thank you for another letter. Your writing speaks from an insightful place. I've recognized this in you before, especially when you dance. Canada was great.

Autumn

Autumn's comments:

Omari knows where he's going; I can only respect that. I'll admit that this move to Atlanta leaves me uneasy. I know Black men like those big booty girls! My competition in the Northwest is nothing, but it's hard to stand up and block trade when you're not around.

A Seattle Perspective

Maybe I can persuade Omari to tattoo my name on his butt! Maybe I should start sending him scratch and sniff letters!

When I told my girlfriends that Omari was leaving to live in another city, but we were going to continue our relationship, they went crazy! I felt like a wounded deer in a wolf pack! I was lucky to get out of there alive! However, I have confidence we can make this work. I have confidence Omari loves me. I have confidence in finding the lowest fare to Atlanta, so I can look out after my best interests! Not that I don't trust Omari, but I don't want my "dawg" to start eating out of someone else's bowl!

Omari's comments:

How do you reassure someone when you don't know what the future holds? I feel responsible, since I'm the one making the move. What can I do to soothe Autumn's soul?

Music always soothes my soul, so I put on some Marvin Gaye. I listen as he sings those romantic ballads, "Distant Lover," and "Let's Get It On!" I hear him sing, "Please baby please; I want you to want me." Yeah!

Autumn's Letter:

Omari,

Do you know what I want? I want to wake up in the morning with you next to me. I want to look underneath the covers and see your beautiful body. I want to feel the contrast of your velvet smooth skin and the hardness of your erection. I want to lick your body and watch your expressions, while you succumb to my desire. I want to stand with you in front of the mirror and see our bodies blend as one. I want to hear you say that I'm yours for the taking. I want to make love so passionately that we fall back to sleep.

Autumn

Letters to My Lover

Autumn's comments:
    Hey, I might as well try to stock up on as much good loving as I can. A woman can never have too much of a good "thang"! Anyway, it looks as if trade is ready to come to a screeching halt!

Omari's Comments:
    Damn, Autumn has me ready to make a quick booty run! You know, it's every "dawg's" fantasy to have a woman who acts like a lady in public and a whore in the bedroom!

Chapter Nineteen
What Do You Think of This Idea?

Autumn,
    What do you think of this idea? I want you to travel across the country with me. I remember you telling me that you've never traveled outside the Great Northwest. This'll give you the chance to meet my friends. Will you come? Please say yes!

Omari

Omari's comments:
    I wanna stay relaxed, while on the road. After a hard day's drive, a man needs to have his oil checked.
    Its confession time again. One of the byproducts of dancing, is the luxury of having a woman in every port. So, how do I introduce Autumn? "Hey baby, I'd like you to meet my long lost half-sister. Oh, we don't want to impose on you too much, so I'll just sleep with Autumn tonight! Oh yeah, I forgot to tell you, Autumn likes to pray in the middle of the night. So, don't worry if you hear her saying...Oh God, oh God, yes sweet Jesus, here I cum Lord, here I cum!"

What Do You Think of This Idea?

Autumn's Reply:

Omari,
What an extremely attractive offer, one I can't refuse! I know how you "dawgs" operate. So, what's the exchange? You know I believe in paying my part of the bill!
With an offer like that, I'll have to think of something, to assure you aren't stressed while driving! Omari, you continue to surprise me.

Autumn

Chapter Twenty
Leaving The Big House

I soon realized how much work it was to uproot from one part of the country and relocate to another. The houses acquired in Seattle over the past ten years posed a problem. That was where Leo came to the rescue. He wanted to hang around Seattle for another year before beginning a two-year world tour. You see, Leo was a Renaissance man who didn't stay in one place too long. But, the timing would work out perfectly. He'd oversee more of the restoration of the big house and remain living there until his departure. He'd also manage the other properties. I made arrangements for the renters to direct-deposit their rent payments into a local account. We'd figure out the rest as things progressed (or as Ted Kennedy would say, "I'll cross that bridge when I get to it").

We'd been living in the basement for the prior six months, while reconfiguring the upper floors. The progress was stunning. We took more of the lifting beams and incorporated them into the structure of the building. This opened up the entire floor and gave a large, spatial effect. The living room, dining room and kitchen flowed together to create one large living space. The ceilings were eleven feet high

Letters to My Lover

and all of the original crown molding was saved, refurbished, and reinstalled.

The original house had a big country porch facing the water, supported by ten oak pillars. During the lifting phase, the porch was demolished. This gave us the opportunity to replace it with a beautiful sun-room, consisting of solid glass, facing the lake. We built a grand entrance leading into the sun-room by adding French doors. Now, every room on the main floor had the same stunning view of Lake Washington!

We converted a bedroom into a spacious bathroom and installed a jetted tub with lots of privacy windows. Leo made a design statement with the first floor and to say it was beautiful is an understatement. It was uniquely Leo!

Two days before my scheduled departure, Leo moved into the new space. That gave us the opportunity to rent out the basement (and continue to fund this bad habit).

The next day we held a "good riddance" celebration and invited our friends to visit the house and say goodbye. Everyone who came by saw that the ugly duckling was transforming into something beautiful. I remember one of my "dawgs" proposing a toast.

"This is to Omari and Leo. The only two mutherfuckers that I know who are crazy enough to think of doing some crazy shit like this. To the two mutherfuckers who talked all of their friends into giving free labor, in support of this crazy project. To the two mutherfuckers who're going to pull this off and have their dreams come true. Salute!"

I thought about it for a second and then looked over at Leo. It was now obvious; we were pulling off the impossible!

Leaving the big house felt as if I were walking away from my child. This project had consumed the prior three years of my life and now I was letting go. It was hard, but also liberating. This project had taken so much of my energy, yet sparked my imagination as nothing before.

It was nice to see that our hard work was paying off. A feeling of accomplishment filled my spirit and I remember saying to

Leaving The Big House

Leo, "You always have a place to stay Leo, no matter what. You always have a place you can call home." It felt good to tell my best friend that. Leo's generosity *was* the richest gift that I've ever received in life and his friendship meant the world to me.

    The next morning, with my car packed and heading for Portland to pick up Autumn, I take one last glance at the big house. Breathing deeply, and with many memories, I drive off to begin a new journey.

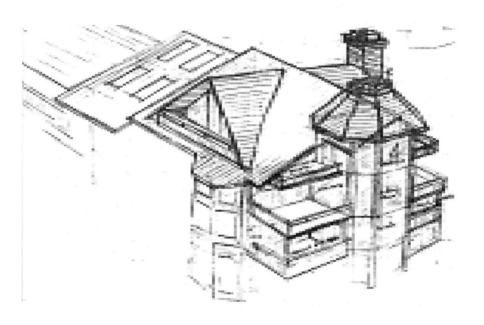

Letters to My Lover

Chapter Twenty-One
Across America Together

Autumn's Letter:

Omari,

    Words can't express what I've experienced over the last two weeks. To be honest, I was apprehensive about traveling; it's something I've never done. Not knowing what to expect made me nervous, but one hundred miles from home, I became fascinated by our adventure. My girlfriends didn't believe me when I told them that we were going dancing across the United States. Taking a picture at every state line was a clever idea.

    Now I understand your gratification when you travel to different places. My strongest impression of the entire trip was meeting your twin brother. You guys are very much alike and share the same mannerisms. Your family traits are very strong; meeting him revealed many things about you. I can't wait to meet the rest of the clan.

    By the time we left California, I was relaxed and enjoying myself. Omari, you are so unpredictable. Deciding to go to Las Vegas (lost wages) on a day's notice to watch the Tyson fight was exciting. I've never gone to a boxing match, nevertheless a gambling casino. The crowd was so intense during the match. I found myself enthralled by it all and confess to getting horny during the fight. Afterwards I wanted you so bad, and to be honest, you were a knockout!

    How did you know it's every woman's fantasy to cross into Mexico and go shopping? Our matching leather outfits are *so* sexy. But the leather jockstrap, come on Omari! Okay, I confess, your leather jock *does* look sexy. But, I think you enjoy that fur lining a little too much!

    Texas is a big place. Don't they make movies about people stuck in the middle of nowhere? I really enjoyed Dallas. Some of those women's jeans were so tight; they looked like walking "sampler plates"! Northwest women are a bit more subtle.

Across America Together

Being in New Orleans and dancing to that Creole music was the best of all. New Orleans is rich with culture and the food was *so* spicy! I hope I didn't keep you awake with my constant reminders of that great meal. I wanted to make sure you got your money's worth! (Although it was making my eyes burn a little!)

When I saw the Atlanta skyline, it was difficult to believe our trip was ending. Omari, you've opened my eyes to a world that I never knew existed. Now I want more!

Autumn

Chapter Twenty-Two
The New Life Begins

Omari's Comments:

Atlanta! I love this city. It's refreshing to be in a city where Black people form the majority. Not one white person has come up to me and asked, "How's it going guy?" You don't know how much I hate hearing that stupid question.

Music saturates the air and Atlanta immediately felt like home. Big booty girls, in every shade of chocolate, are a welcome sight.

Omari's Letter:

Autumn,

It's hard to describe the transformation going on in my head. The change of location is exciting. My assignment in Atlanta is a natural and I've negotiated an operating budget big enough to take care of the company (and make a few deals on the side). One thing I've found out very quickly, when you have access to money, you become very popular! Now I realize why my colleague kept insisting that I take the assignment.

There must be something in the water down here because

Letters to My Lover

kids are everywhere. Everyone asks me, "Why don't you have a couple of kids? Is something wrong?" I tell them, "Where I'm from, we use something called birth control!" It's obvious I'm in the Deep South because the other day, "Billy-Bob" introduced me to his wife and sister, but there was only one woman standing there! It took me a while to figure out that one. Yep, I've stumbled into more interactive theater and I have a role to play, whether I want it or not!

Omari

Reality is a Mother!

Omari's comments:
        For an art project, I've decided to take a picture a day of anything capturing my interest. In a grocery store, I see a brother wearing leather pants with the butt cut out. No kidding, the butt is gone! He's also sporting a gold chain, which runs from his zipper to his nose! I follow him for a while, because he's a perfect candidate for the picture of the day!
        The brotha's walking around asking everyone for money. I notice all the White people avoid eye contact and immediately change directions to evade this guy. When he approaches a Black person, they look at him as if he's crazy and tell him to go away! When he walks up to me, I say, "Man your ass is hanging out of your pants, can't you feel that? You're gonna get your drawers dirty!" He looks at me and asks, "Brother, ya got a tip?" First, I ask to take his picture. After I get my picture, I tell him my tip is to take some of the money he's bumming off people and get the ass sewed into his pants! Of course, he didn't appreciate my suggestion. He starts to come closer, until I inform him of the large personal space that I require, and if he invades it, he'll find out what it feels like to have a gold chain extricated from this nose quicker than he can sneeze! He stops and tells me, "The boys think my pants are sexy!" The conversation abruptly ended! However, I did get my picture for the day.

Chapter Twenty-Three
A Black Man's Perspective

Black people in America are identifiable, and to think that Blackness is not an identifiable feature is a fallacy. People by nature identify others by their unique characteristics and color is a reference point. The way people are treated, once identified by their unique characteristic, is the point of this discussion.

If a person perceives another in a stereotypical fashion, the encounter can be a negative experience for both people. Hence, being Black and associated with only the negative consequences is a negative experience, plain and simple.

My preference is to call this an "ism," it's different from racism, sexism, or classism. We all do it, so it's difficult to say that one particular race participates more often in these "isms" than another. Yet, when it happens to us as individuals, we don't like it.

In the heart of the South, certain aspects of American culture become very clear. For example, it's obvious that the American tradition primarily benefits the white male and his stock. Additionally, "America's stock" interprets and projects Black people in a way that justifies our exploitation. Being in the South allows me to realize that the things around me don't necessarily take into account the interest of my well-being. I also understand that I'm integrated within a culture that treats me like a second-class citizen, yet I still have a need to look for a personal identity within that culture.

When I explore the question of America's "ism," I'm beset by conflict. It's a conflict within me *and* with the public's perception of me. Why is it when a Black person articulates an African American position, it strikes the uninformed observer as a phenomena?

Exploring our Black race, I see a myriad of styles and I know the Black aesthetic exists. When I submerge myself deep into *my* surroundings, I experience a personal and profound sense of being and self-worth. Living in the south, I see how important it is for us to begin to address each other with a style and dignity that acknowledges *our* creativity and *our* beauty as *we* see it.

Letters to My Lover

Autumn's comments:

Omari shares his thoughts in our phone conversations. I can tell he's growing by leaps and bounds. Of course, the thought entered my mind that he might leap out of my life.

We've written daily letters for the last few months. I know the "dawg" needs to hunt because it's in his blood. That concerns me. I'm also in need of an "oil change"! My friends tell me, "Autumn get a hold of yourself," then I confess, "That's all I ever do!" Maybe it's time for the doctor to make a house call.

Chapter Twenty-Four
Angela

A few of my colleagues at work began to express concern for me. We went out socially at least once a week, but since Omari's departure, they were seeing less of me. I was suffering a little bit of an emotional letdown. Angela decided that she was tired of watching me wallow in self-pity.

Angela was a different sort of woman who marched to her own drumbeat. She was an attorney who brought many of her own clients with her when she joined our firm two years ago. Her niche was the music industry. Her connections brought a constant revenue stream to the firm and garnered personal invitations to meet most of the musicians coming through Portland. Angela was thirty-five, stood about five feet ten, inches tall, and wouldn't even consider dating a man less than six feet tall, or someone making less than a million dollars a year. Color didn't matter to Angela, as long as the color of his money was green. She was a cunning woman with one glaring character flaw; she'd go through men like water leaking from a rusty bucket. She didn't mind meeting someone on Friday and jumping into bed with them before the stroke of midnight. At our Monday staff meetings, she'd tell me about her "weekend conquests". This small flaw, coupled with the fact that most of the men she met were associated with the music industry, were the equivalent of drinking

Angela

and driving. Every couple of weeks, Angela's life had some type of drama going on. It took her about two days to get over one romance, before she'd go chasing the next.

Closing a contract representing yet another music industry client, everyone decided to get together on Saturday to celebrate. "Girl, you've got to come to this set. There'll be some seriously sharp brothers showing up, throwing around lots of cash. They'll be looking for someone to spend it on. I know you've been singing the blues, so come on along and have some fun. I'll pick you up at 10:00 p.m., sharp."

Chapter Twenty-Five
Still Gotta Dance

Its early evening when we finish having dinner with some out of town clients who are trying to secure some work with the company; wining and dining is always a good starting point.

Walking to the car, I pass the window of a dance studio and watch for a few minutes, as some brothers' step off their dance routines. These guys are combining jazz with urban steps - all behind some funky rhythms. It looks great! Of course, I want to meet them. I needed some help getting plugged into the local dance scene.

I open the door and a bell rings, signaling my entry. A beautiful woman in workout clothes comes toward me, wiping her forehead with a towel. "Can I help you?"

"Hello, my name's Omari. I was checking out the brothers through the window and wondering if the "doctors" work on emergency cases. You see, I have two left feet!"

Before entering the place, I'd taken my shoes off and placed them on the wrong feet. Wanting to meet these guys, I thought they'd get a kick out of a brother acting so crazy! (But I wasn't going to cut the ass out of my pants!) When she looks down at my feet, she bursts out laughing.

Letters to My Lover

"Hello, my name is Cherish. Looks like you need a miracle more than dance lessons! I'm sure they won't mind if you come in and take a seat." I can tell by the eagerness on her face that she wants to recruit another paying customer. My lack of a southern accent reveals that I'm not a local. Her eyes follow, as she directs me to a seat. (It's hard to walk with my shoes on the wrong feet.)

"Please don't disturb the guys and speak with me before you leave." Cherish walks away, still chuckling that I'd come in with my shoes on the wrong feet. She makes it a point to show me that she isn't wearing a wedding ring, putting an extra wiggle in her step on her way out.

The three brothers look over at the corner. I've encroached upon their creative space. I lift my hand in a gesture of appreciation, for allowing me to watch. Their combination of unique styles and music is an entertaining sight. Rarely do you find young brothers with an affinity for the jazz masters. They're swinging to Count Basie's "One O'clock Jump". These guys take the music to another level with their moves. Dizzy Gillespie stated that, "A true artist must first have command of his instrument." It was obvious; these brothers *were* in total control of their bodies. They look to be in their mid-twenties and in top condition.

The Count begins a piano solo and the first dancer steps to the center, tilting his hat. Stepping double-time to the music, he's cool as cool can be. The band comes in after sixteen bars; the other two dancers begin a synchronized lindy-hop in the background. They keep their eyes on each other, and while one flips to his hands, the other grabs his ankles. Eddie "Lockjaw" Davis begins blowing his solo, as they barrel-roll across the floor. Hopping to their feet and running full speed, they slid across the floor, lining up behind the first dancer; throwing in hip-hop moves with their upper bodies. The middle dancer careens over the head of the front dancer, extending his legs and touching his toes, displaying his strength and flexibility. He gyrates his hips at lightning speed, in a masculine, sexual motion. The last dancer runs and slides through his legs and comes up tap dancing. All of this is going at breakneck speed with "One O'clock Jump" wailing

Still Gotta Dance

in the background! After the song is over, they animatedly discuss their routine and then start up again.

After an hour of constant motion, the guys finally take a break. I introduce myself, letting them know that I'm not just a pedestrian off the street, but a fellow artist who appreciates their art form. Informing them of my African dance background, I ask if they feel comfortable having some different energy entering their circle. They ask me to come back the following evening and bring my dance shoes. (On the proper feet, of course.)

The prospect of dancing with such dynamic, young, creative brothers is exciting. One of the reasons that my career had lasted so long is my approach to dancing. Whenever I'm in the studio, I'm there solely to work. My contribution to these brothers would be to show them some African steps and see if they wanted to incorporate a different style into their dancing.

After the first night, they ask me to come back. Soon, we're working out regularly. Dancing with these guys is inspiring and it feels great being back in the dance studio. I offer Cherish some business and marketing tips to help bring in more students. Teaching a Saturday morning African dance class in exchange for studio time brings in new students. Cherish invites a master drummer named Hamet to drum for the class. The class becomes so popular; we must limit its size. After class, Hamet walks out with cash in hand; it's obvious, he likes the job.

Hamet observes our evening session with the guys. After watching our routines, he immediately offers his services, along with some other top-notch drummers. Live drummers put the icing on our cake!

Within two months of walking into the dance studio and making a fool of myself, we'd assembled an all-male music and dance troupe. Our creative energy (and testosterone) is undeniable.

Cherish lines up a couple of performance dates. Together, we bring a power and energy to the stage that blows audiences away! Cherish quickly books us on a local television program. After our appearance, the phone in the dance studio never quits ringing!

Letters to My Lover

The move to Atlanta is beginning to offer unique opportunities and I'm determined to take full advantage. The people tapping off my creative energies in Seattle are gone. In Atlanta, any part of my personality is free to emerge. The uncertainty and apprehension of moving into unknown territory is quickly replaced with a renewed sense of confidence. The move is rapidly improving my quality of life.

Chapter Twenty-Six
Poetry in Motion

It's Saturday evening and I'm having trouble deciding what to wear to the party. I must've changed clothes ten different times, going from business attire to something a little sexier; after all, it *was* a party. I feel a little awkward about hanging out with Angela. She didn't invite the rest of our gang to the party - only me.

One thing about Angela – she's always on time. For her, time is money and she doesn't like anyone wasting her money. The doorbell rings precisely at 10:00 p.m. I open the door and there stands Angela, poured into a black dress, showing *all* her curves *and* those long legs! The dress stops about two inches below her ass. To make matters worse, she sporting spiked heels that make her six inches taller! "Hey girl, you ready to party?" Angela steps inside and shuts the door. "Angela, I thought this was a business party."

"Girl, there'll be some nice-looking men at this party. I just want to look my best. Tonight I want to be entertained." I can't help but laugh, knowing she's up to no good. With tires screeching, we speed off in Angela's "boy-toy," a Mercedes 450 SL.

Arriving at the downtown Hilton, Angela pulls in for the valet to park the car. We step out and the valet's tongue falls out of his mouth. "Good evening, ladies! Our crew will provide you 'special service'. Here's my card. When you're ready to leave, call me. Your car will be waiting." The valet looks at Angela from head to toe. His look implies, "I'll give you special service and later on, you give me special service." Angela plays along and winks back with a suggestive look that says, "Take care of my car and later on, I'll take care of you!" I scowl at Angela. "Don't start something that's going to get us in trouble!" Angela laughs, "Girlfriend, I'm just getting warmed up!"

The firm reserved the Hilton penthouse suite for the evening. We enter the lobby of the hotel and take the elevator to the twenty-fifth floor. A tuxedoed door attendant greets us with a tip of his hat. He also gives Angela that head–to-toe look. She wiggles her body and tugs at her hemline, moving it down an inch. The door opens and she walks into the room as if she owns the hotel.

"Angela!" Someone shouts as we enter the room. They greet each other with a hug and kiss. "Congratulations on the new account, and who's this beautiful lady you've brought?"

"Good evening, my name's Autumn." I extended my hand. Ignoring my gesture, he grabs me and insists on a kissing my cheek. "Good evening, Autumn, my name's Marcus. Welcome to the party." By that introduction, I can tell Marcus is part of the L.A. contingent. I can also tell that he's well on his way to having a good time. His breath reeks of liquor. "Make yourself at home. If you need anything (or anyone), just let me know." Angela and Marcus snuggle up for a talk. I take a stroll around the room.

This may have been Angela's element, but it sure isn't mine. In an effort to look busy and not feel so awkward, I help myself to the nice spread of food. A nice-looking gentleman walks by and stops. "Excuse me, may I sit with you?" I look up. "Oops, I don't mean to hog the whole table! Please sit down."

"I saw you piling up that plate and thought it might be a good idea to get in there, before *all* the shrimp are gone. Hello, my name's Cheye. I'm playing in the band. Someone must've gotten paid, because they're serving more than just rubber chicken!" His offbeat, clever manner lightens the air. "My name's Autumn, I work with the firm. It's a pleasure to meet you."

"How come you're not mingling like the rest of the people? Weren't you in on the deal?" Cheye inquires. "Angela's the brain behind this deal. I'm just along for the ride. It gives me the chance to

Letters to My Lover

eat up all the shrimp." I can tell by Cheye's reaction to my remark that he's probing me. "Is Angela the tall lady sporting that beautiful black dress?" This gives me the idea that he and Angela might have something in common. Like chasing the money, (or the honey). "Yep, that's Angela. We're running buddies."

Watching Angela is like watching poetry in motion. The girl has the perfect body for that dress and she knows it! Within an hour of stepping into the room, she has every man wrapped around her finger. She isn't shy about hugging and kissing either. Men, married or single, like that. It's part of her game. Angela prides herself on being able to stay a few steps ahead of the person she's trying to hustle.

Cheye's a piano player and listening to him play is a pleasure. His "smooth jazz" style creates the perfect atmosphere for the evening. Sitting in the corner, I shut my eyes, hoping the music would take me to another place. I imagine Omari stepping through the doors. Dressed in a tuxedo, he announces to the party that he wants to perform a special dance, just for me.

Angela's laugh brings me back to reality. "How are you doing girlfriend? Are you having a good time?" She continues to laugh. Marcus is following her around like a puppy. The alcohol has him thinking that he has a chance to see what's under that body wrap. Angela's smarter than that. Girlfriend doesn't give up the booty for free. There's always a price to pay, also, Angela gets paid in advance. She pulls me close. "We're thinking about heading out of here and checking out another party. Wanna come along?" Immediately, Marcus suggests that one of his friends join us, to make it a foursome. That determines my answer. "No, I'm having a good time listening to the music. I'm gonna hang out a while, then go home."

Angela whispers in my ear. "Hey girlfriend, enjoy yourself. These interesting men came up from L.A. to celebrate our newfound relationship. We're going to be seeing more of each other over the next year. It's always nice to meet new friends, so relax. Don't put your life on hold."

Extending my hand for her keys, "I'll need your car to get

Poetry in Motion

home." Angela looks annoyed. "That's right, we *did* come together." Marcus butts in, "No problem. We've got a limousine outside waiting for us. Autumn can take your car, don't worry, *I'll drive you home.*" The emphasis on his final words weren't unnoticed. Angela and I glance at each other. I'm worried for her safety. She gives me the eye to let me know that she's in control of the situation. "Here's the keys, don't wreck it! I'll call you tomorrow." I sense the authority in her voice. Yep, she's in control.

The band's taking a break and I thank Cheye for his music. "You're not leaving so soon are you? The night's still young."

"The night's young for musicians. We working people turn into sleepy heads around midnight." I begin walking toward the door. "Autumn, I'm working another party next week. Will you come and be my cheering section?" Cheye hands me his business card. "Well, I don't...." He doesn't allow me time to refuse. "Please." Giving me that, "I'll be heartbroken, if you don't accept my offer" look. I take is card, "Let me think about it."

Riding the elevator to the lobby, I reflect on the interesting evening. Watching Angela hustle men is such a contrast to watching her at work.

Walking out of the hotel, I signal the valet for the car. When he notices that I'm alone, his reaction changes. It was if Angela had personally insulted this guy, by not electing to go home with him. "That'll be ten dollars please." He looks at me with rejection in his eyes. If Angela were here, no money would exchange hands, only innuendoes. However, I'm not Angela. Handing him ten dollars, he opens the door; again finding his professional etiquette. Adjusting the seat, I realize its Angela's long legs that provoke men into acting like "dawgs". The sight of a sexy woman driving a 450 SL, only adds to the allure. Sliding Cheye's card in my purse, I put the top down to begin the drive home.

Letters to My Lover

Chapter Twenty-Seven
It's Hot!

This is the disk jockey at WFUNK and it's hot outside! The weather is so hot that they've issued a "bad hair day" alert! Due to the overflow of heat related victims in the emergency room, they've asked all the "well-endowed" ladies not to wear their black outfits to the bus stop. It's so hot, even the Muslims have taken off their suit jackets and unbuttoned their bow ties. Stay inside folks, cuz it's hot in "Hot-lanta" today!

Chapter Twenty-Eight
Arnett Howard's Creole Funk Band

The heat makes it a perfect night to run the streets and listen to some music. A few of the dancers were going to the Midtown dance hall to check out a hot new band in town called, "Arnett Howard's Creole Funk Band".

It feels good running the streets and getting into the mix of things. About a block away from the club, I hear a trumpet going to town! He has a New Orleans swing "thang" going on. I walk into the dance hall just as he's finishing his tune and the place is already rocking!

"I'd like to introduce ourselves, my name is Arnett Howard, and we're the Creole Funk Band." He acknowledges me, as I finish paying the cover charge. "Another paying customer, come on in! Hey brotha, do me a favor, step on over to the dance floor and grab a few of these pretty women. It looks like there's a shortage of men to take care of these ladies needs." I look over to see a surplus of beautiful women, ready and willing to take on all participants. I shout back to Arnett, "No problem brotha!"

Arnett's energy is contagious and his personality makes you feel good! "How yaw feeling tonight?" The crowd reacts with a

Arnett Howard's Creole Funk Band

thunderous roar. He starts his next song. Two women grab me at the same time, neither willing to give any ground to the other. In these awkward predicaments, my unwritten rule is to dance with the ugly one first; that way everyone knows you're an "equal opportunity dawg". But there's nothing ugly on either of these women. Luckily, Arnett notices my predicament and shouts over the mike, "Come on, brother. Get 'em' both on the dance floor!" Now that's a true "dawg" barking!

The band's playing a curious mix of Creole, funk, and reggae. Arnett's out front directing this energetic show. This guy is multi-talented. He's playing the keyboards and singing, seemingly making up the words as he goes along. He points over to us and begins to sing.

"The brotha walks in, just loving the space.
Seeing beautiful women all over the place.
He grabs two and gets on the floor.
Looks like soon he's gonna need two more!"

Arnett grabs his trumpet and heads onto the dance floor. He's blowing a New Orleans rag over the top of this funky rhythm. He comes over to the three of us, who by now have commandeered our own section of the dance floor. "Take 'em' to the bridge, brotha," Arnett shouts. His trumpet belts out a sound so funky, it has me throwing booty around like there's no tomorrow! Arnett grabs one of the women and blows his horn at her feet, making her dance. Still playing the trumpet, he begins to dance! This guy's creative energy has no limit. Finally, he spins the woman back in my direction and dances off, still wailing on the trumpet! You couldn't help but be infected with this guy's energy!

Arnett steps back on stage, still directing the band. He ends the song with a long trumpet solo, hitting all the high notes! The audience gives him a standing ovation!

The guy has everyone on the dance floor sweating like hell! What an act! Arnett Howard and his Creole Funk Band.

Letters to My Lover

Chapter Twenty-Nine
I'm Bored!

It's Friday afternoon and I'm bored stiff. All the briefs for the next week's court schedule have been filed, and there's still two hours remaining before quitting time. I shut the door to try to get some homework done, but I don't want to study. I'm thinking, "Maybe I should take Cheye up on his offer and go to his party." Every time I start to dial the number on his card, guilt makes me hang up. Calling Cheye and getting the time and location of his gig is harmless. So why am I acting like this? Picking up the phone, I hit re-dial and take a deep breath. "Greetings, this is Cheye, and unfortunately, I'm not here to answer your call. If you're calling to book the band, please call Trident Entertainment at 503-972-5520. We're playing a private party on Friday and Saturday we're at the Plaza Ballroom beginning at 10:00 p.m. If ya want to be added to our mailing list, please leave your name and address. Otherwise, leave a message and your phone call will be returned. Peace." Hanging up without leaving a message, I'm mad at myself for feeling so guilty. Hitting re-dial again, I wait to leave a message. "Hi Cheye, this is Autumn. I met you at the Hilton last week. I'm calling to say hello and to see if your offer to come watch the band still stands. I'm in and out all the time, so I'll call you later and try to speak with you in person. Hope all is well. Goodbye."

A minute later, the phone rings. It's Cheye. "Hello Autumn, this is Cheye, I notice you just called." His voice sounds eager to talk. "How did you get my number?"

"Sorry, I have caller I.D. When I heard your voice, I immediately called back. I hope you don't mind." He sounds genuine. "How are you?" Replying, somewhat unnerved. "Now that I hear your voice, I feel great! Do you wanna accompany me to the party tonight? I'd love for ya to come." I'm feeling somewhat flattered that he sounds so eager to see me. "What type of party is it?"

"I'm not really sure, but it's at the Wiltshire Country Club. I suspect it's some rich White folks, just wanting some background music. Odds are we'll be the only Black people around. Please

I'm bored!

come and save me from boredom." We both laugh. "I know where the Wiltshire Country Club is. What time do you start?"

"Dinner starts at seven and we begin playing at nine. We play for an hour then we're done. *I promise to have you in bed by eleven.*" Cheye's remark had a certain smirk in it. I think for a moment. "Okay, I'll come, where shall we meet?"

"It might be best if we arrive together. I can meet you some place and we'll drive one car." I'm thinking of my safety and didn't like the idea of being a captive audience. "How about we meet downtown and I'll follow you? Let's say, the Red Cat Café, at eight o'clock sharp."

"That'll work. The others are arriving earlier to set up the equipment. We can just walk in. It's a date, the Red Cat Café at eight, see you there." Cheye hangs up the phone.

I wasn't bored anymore. Cheye called it a date, but I'm going because I like his music. Maybe I should've made that clear.

Chapter Thirty
Religion

In the Deep South, religion plays a central part in the social fabric of the society. The things that I'm experiencing reaffirm my faith in The Creator. I've always enjoyed going to church and have this curious fascination between performance and faith. Preaching has a sense of rhythm to it. Can I get an Amen!

A colleague invited me to attend his local church. On this particular Sunday, the preacher delivers a sermon that fills the place with electricity! Some of the people (who were sinning like there was no tomorrow the night before) are high on Jesus. The first act of this play brings out *all* the performers. Can I get an Amen!

The preacher feels the beat of the crowd and begins to preach his gospel. Sitting in the audience, I watch in amazement as the minister works his crowd into a fever pitch. He's conducting a concert and everyone enjoys the gospel emulating from the pulpit. I can feel the energy in the air. Suddenly, the Holy Spirit engulfs everything along its path. The preacher shouts, "Do you feel it? I said do you feel it?" Can I get an Amen!

The preacher wants my soul (along with a healthy contribution to the "Building Fund"). He preaches as the choir sings. The roof is rocking and my knees are knocking. He shouts, "We're all be bums when the devil comes." Man, this place is jumping! Can I get an Amen!

Near the end of the service, the preacher calls out for anyone wanting to surrender his or her life to The Creator. As the people go forward (mostly women), a young man walks towards the pulpit seemingly consumed by the devil? His body contorts as everyone prays for his soul. The choir is singing, as the young man's body writhes. I watch in morbid fascination, while this surreal event unfolds before my eyes. What's going on in his man's head? Can it be real?

The preacher saves the young man's soul, delivering another soldier to The Creator, (or at least bringing the poor boy back to his senses). The preacher ends his sermon with a prayer. I observe the men looking at their watches, hoping not to miss too much of the big game. Feeling redeemed, (for another week) I'm ready to tackle the obstacles that lay ahead. **Can I get an Amen!**

Chapter Thirty-One
The Second Year

Autumn

Two years and we're still going strong. What's next? Our five-year anniversary? Is that where we turn into blimps, lose all of our teeth, and go around scratching our butts in front of each other? Now *that's* true romance!

Omari

Friday Night

Chapter Thirty-Two
Friday Night

Before calling it a day, I buzzed Angela's office to tell her about my phone call to Cheye. "Girlfriend, live a little!" She said, with her sly laugh. I swiftly reply, "It's boredom more than anything else. Anyway, his music sounds nice, so I called him. He's invited me to watch his set tonight."

"Have fun girl; you need to get out more. A little advice though, you have to watch those musicians; they're a different breed. The other night, Marcus tried everything to get under my dress! I had to let him know that we've worked too long on this deal to mess it up by mixing business with pleasure. In reality, I ran a financial report on him and the brotha doesn't have the financial resources to afford a woman like me. That makes things easy; we're all business and no pleasure! But, I'll give him ten points for trying. We had a nice time after the party. I'll see you at Monday staff and we'll compare notes."

Arriving at the Red Cat Café, I see Cheye walking in. Pulling over and blowing my horn, he turns around to see me waving.

"Hey Autumn. I'm parked around the corner. Will ya take me to the van?" Cheye jumps in the car. "It's good to see you again. I'm glad you called. You look beautiful." He would've kept going, if I hadn't cut him off at the pass. "Okay, enough with the compliments. I wanted to get out of the house and listening to your music is a good excuse. Thanks for the invite." We pull up to his van. "I'll follow you." I can tell that Cheye's annoyed by my insistence on taking two cars.

We pull into the country club. A young man, smartly dressed, parks our cars. We share a friendly hug. "So, we meet again young lady." I can tell by his voice and hug that we need to communicate, just to get things straight. He escorts me inside.

"Nice thing about these gigs is they feed ya. Oh yeah, that's how we met, fighting over a bowl of shrimp!" Cheye continues, "Here I am with a beautiful woman, a nice meal and at the end of the night;

Letters to My Lover

I'm walking out with a check! This must be heaven!" We both give a shallow laugh.

Something about Cheye's conversation told me that he likes being in control. He chatters constantly about little things. He *was* an entertainer and maybe he's only trying to entertain.

"Cheye let me be up front with you so you don't get the wrong impression. I *have* a boyfriend. I love and respect him. He's out of town. I just wanted to get out of the house and relax for the evening. You present yourself as a gentleman and that's why I called. I enjoy your music and appreciate that you've invited me." I pretend to smile, just to make sure that my words aren't too direct. He smiles back, but I see the disappointment in his eyes.

"That's the story of my life. You beautiful women are already spoken for." I jokingly remind him of all the tipsy women that throw themselves at piano players. "How come every piano player tries to use the same pick-up-line? Here's to the beautiful woman sitting over in the corner. (Getting drunk alone!) I wrote this tune this afternoon and dedicate it to you." It's a weak joke, but it keeps the tension down.

Hanging out with Cheye and listening to the band is different. I'm glad I found enough nerve to make the call. It was turning out to be a nice evening. The band plays one long set, then quits.

"Cheye, thank you for a beautiful evening." I give him a hug. "Hey, you're not going home already are you? The night's still young. Let's go have a cup of coffee somewhere." He didn't want the evening to end. "Again, thanks for a beautiful evening, but I'm going home. Will you walk me to my car?" He puts his arm around me. "Well, I don't care what you say, this *was* a date!" Cheye tries to lighten the atmosphere, as he opens the car door.

"Yes, this was a nice date." I start my engine. "Can I get your number?" He gives me that sad puppy look again. "Hey, let's not complicate things. Maybe, I'll call your number and find out where you're playing again."

Driving off, I see him waving goodbye in the rearview mirror. "You know I'll call you back!"

Friday Night

Omari's thoughts:
A combination of missing Autumn and looking at all these beautiful chocolate women down here has this "dawg" barking big time! Let me write my baby a sexy letter. Just to let her know that I'm still strong (yet, getting weak in the knees and dribbling down my chin). Down boy!

Chapter Thirty-Three
Sexy Dreams

Autumn,
I've been having a recurring dream. Each time we talk, it adds another chapter. It's so vivid, I decided to write it down, and it goes something like this...

You wake to a sunny morning and realize you're on a cruise ship. You're going to Jamaica to meet your husband-to-be, a match made by your mother. You haven't officially met this guy, but you do know that he's rich. The idea of having your mother pick your future husband makes you feel a little uneasy.

Since you're on this nice cruise, and indulging in good food is part of the fun, you get dressed to go up for breakfast. Later, you'll take in some sun on the deck. On your way to breakfast, you notice that a newlywed couple occupies the cabin next door. Passing by, you hear laughing, in your mind's eye you ask, "Wonder what they're doing."

Sitting alone at a table for two, you hear a voice. "Excuse me; may I join you for breakfast?" You look up to see a handsome young man wearing a robe over a bikini. "Please, have a seat." He introduces himself, "Hello my name's Omari." Carrying *The Wall Street Journal,* he puts it aside to talk with you.

After a pleasant conversation, you excuse yourself. Omari gives his thanks for allowing him to be your breakfast companion. In the back of your mind, you're thinking, "It'd be nice if we crossed paths before the end of the cruise." However, your conscience says, "I can't talk to this guy. I don't know much about him and I'm on my way to get married."

Back in your cabin, you get dressed in your two-piece swimsuit. A final look in the mirror, you realize your future husband will enjoy "the package".

Meanwhile, in the cabin next door, the laughing and giggling are replaced with deep sighs and urgent voices. "Yes — yes, right there. Oh, you know what I like!" You think to yourself, "Why go to breakfast, when you're living off love!"

Their dance turns rhythmic and you hear the beat. Love making has a unique rhythm all its own and the sounds resonate through your cabin. You have a front row seat. Witnessing this feast, through to its climactic conclusion. The tension releases; next come screams, which may be either of pain or of pleasure. The intense contractions of love express their passion. Then there's silence.

You've been up against the wall, eavesdropping on their game of love. Stepping back to regain your senses, you look down and realize that you're wet.

A quick shower and a little more suntan lotion, then you're ready for some sun. This relaxing time gives you a chance to think about your future husband.

While on the deck, who should walk by but Omari, the gentleman from breakfast. Those cute buns are tucked tightly in his trunks. Behind him, you see a couple of older women. One remarks to the other, "I'm going to try some of that brown sugar before I get off this boat, even if I have to put it on my charge card!" You say to yourself, "Life's short. I can't let this man get away from me. This might be my "Last Tango in Paris!" You get up and tell those women in a cavalier, yet assertive voice, You better leave that brown sugar alone before you get into more than you can handle."

Omari, sitting by himself and finishing his newspaper, casually observes the situation. He wants to talk with you again and is impressed that you've asserted yourself. You see him admiring your bathing suit. You think to yourself, "This guy's kind of cute. I've had enough sun.

Sexy Dreams

Let me persuade Omari into coming back to my cabin. I want his opinion about arranged marriages."

You pass the newlyweds door, bringing back memories of their recent encounter. Settling back in your cabin, you ask Omari his opinion regarding arranged marriages. "Wow, what a situation. Are you ready?" He sees the tension in your face and offers a back message. He hits that spot in the back of your neck where you carry stress. Omari asks about your impending marriage. You sigh as you feel the tension release. "What have I gotten myself into? I'm nervous as hell!"

He surveys your body, as if looking over the table of contents in a book. "I want her to realize the answer's in her mind," he mutters to himself. He moves down your neck, towards your back, knowing the answers to your questions are no further away than his fingertips. "Relax. The answer will come to you." His fingers move down to the small of your back, you let out a soft moan, signaling that the right spots are being touched. You realize, "This man's allowing me to see that the excitement isn't getting to the end. The real excitement is living as much life as possible along the way. The answer *is* at his fingertips."

Feeling a heavy burden lift from your shoulders, you turn over and give Omari a hug. Recalling the couple next door, you let out a sly laugh, knowing this moment may never come again.

Omari

Autumn's comments:

So, Omari wants to have some "letter sex!" Well, what you're about to read has been toned down to protect the faint at heart. I'm thinking of getting on an airplane, hand delivering this letter, butt naked, oiled down, and ready to rumble!

Women can sense when it's time to feed the "dawg". In fact, both of us are ready for some red meat!

Letters to My Lover

Autumn's Reply:

Omari,

Your dream felt so real that I found myself living the experience. After reading your letter, I begin drifting off. So, the story continues...

Feeling that a heavy burden's been lifted from my mind, I turn over and give you a big hug. A thought goes through my mind, "I'm still traveling, aren't I?"

After a warm embrace, I look deep into your eyes and confess. "Omari, I'm burning with desire for you! Give me an experience that will last a lifetime." You tenderly embrace me and confess, "I'm a little nervous, but what a great idea."

Your lips brush against my lobes. You hold me firmly, yet gently. My breasts press against your chest. You push against my legs and I feel you getting hard. Your erection feels so good! I feel your breath on my neck. Your touch sends shivers down my spine. I hear you say, "Sitting here beside you, look what you do to me." You move my hand to your crotch. You're big and hard against my palm. I caress you through your bikini. Kissing me gently, your tongue begins dancing with mine. Massaging my breasts, you roll my nipples between your fingers, making them rise. I groan, as you fumble with my top. Standing up, I undress before you.

Wrapped in each other's arms, we lie down. Looking deep into each other's eyes, we begin our journey to ecstasy. Starting with my neck and moving down to one breast at a time, you suck and bite my nipples, mixing pain with pleasure. Staring into my eyes, you continue licking. Your tongue delves into my navel. My head rolls back. I'm warm and moist. My smell brings out more of the animal in you.

Thinking of the newlyweds next door, I realize they have nothing on us. You're awakening my emotions and bringing out desires in me that I've never experienced before. Yes, I'm being taken, but you're gentle, tending to my every need. Vaguely, I remember you groaning in a low voice.

There is nothing I can do but give you what you want. Reaching

Sexy Dreams

that ultimate feeling, I'm intense with contractions. You give me a series of short, deep thrusts. It feels so good! I feel one more orgasm coming. We laugh as we collapse together. Our entangled bodies smell like hot, sweaty, sex. "What a dream come true!" I feel myself fading...

My sleep is deep and restful. I've never felt like this before, there's no tension, no anxieties. In the distance, I hear a foghorn; it's the call to port. My new beginning. The thought of stopping along the road of life and appreciating the moment with no regrets leaves me content.

Ring... The clock goes off, waking me up. Looking over at the nightstand, my dream is in the letter written to you before I fell asleep. Reading it one more time, I tingle at the thought of loving you.
Autumn

Omari's comments:

I must've read Autumn's letter a hundred times, always before going to bed. Now, I know why men sleep better on their sides than women — because we have a kick-stand!

Autumn's comments:

I realize my last letter was somewhat steamy, but never in my wildest imagination did I expect Omari to send me a pubic hair! I'll cherish it forever.

Chapter Thirty-Four
Perception and Reality

This long distance relationship is getting to me. Portland to Seattle wasn't that bad, but living in opposite ends of the country is a different story. I'm beginning to miss male companionship.

Angela eagerly tells me about her weekend conquests at our

Letters to My Lover

Monday tag-ups. Jokingly, I suggest that she write her memoirs regarding her escapades and entitle it, "Send me to the Moon (one inch at a time)!" We laugh, but she keeps saying the same old thing. "I'm putting my life on hold," and for what? I feel a need to defend myself. "Let's talk about you girl. I'm perfectly happy with my situation."

Cheye's card is still in my desk. Another week comes and goes. Boredom again is knocking on my door. I make the phone call to see if Cheye will rescue me.

"Hello Cheye, its Autumn and this time I'll leave a message. I'm calling to say hello and see if you're playing anywhere around town. I'll call back later"

Angela stops by before heading out to begin her weekend. "Hey girl, don't do anything that I wouldn't do, but I'm going to do it!" She's trying to secure the account of her latest victim, a hunk playing for the Los Angeles Lakers. Her last remark before leaving makes me laugh. "This weekend is about a good time, not a long time!" I roll my eyes and tell her to be safe.

Calling Cheye's number one more time before calling it quits, he answers. "Hello Cheye, this is Autumn." There's a small pause. "Autumn, it's good to hear from you again. I was hoping that you'd call back. Sorry I missed ya the first time.

"What are ya doing tonight? You know that I wanna see ya again. Do ya wanna hang out?" His persistence is a little annoying, but Omari's "letter sex" has left me with energy to burn. Going out to listen to some music is a good way to channel this nervous energy. "Are you playing anywhere?"

"We've got the night off, but I'm going to check out one of my partners. He's playing the cocktail hour right across the street from our office. Do ya wanna check out the first set? I know Cinderella likes to be in bed by eleven. *I'll make sure you're there by then.*"

"Sure I'll come, but just for one set. Where do you want to meet?" Cheye responds quickly. "How about here at the office? That way, we can just walk across the street. We have private parking and that'll save ya eight bucks." I hesitate for a moment. Is this a

Perception and Reality

good idea? "Where're you located?" He clears his throat. "We're on the corner of First and Main in the Plaza building, suite 103." I know the location. "Okay, I'll meet you at seven."

Going home for a quick rest and a change of clothes, I feel a little uneasy. Maybe I should ask my sister if she wants to come along. Should I wear jeans or a dress? Thinking the cosmopolitan look is more appropriate for downtown, I select a dress.

Pulling into the parking lot, I take a deep breath before exiting the car. Here it is, suite 103. I ring the buzzer. The door opens and Cheye greets me with open arms. Autumn! He gives me a strong hug. I tentatively hug back. "Hello Cheye."

"You look beautiful!" Putting my hands on my hips and playfully saying, "Hey, haven't we been through this before?" He laughs. "You still look beautiful and you wore a dress, just for me!" His insistence that I've gone through some extra effort, just for him strikes a nerve. "Thanks Cheye, do you like it?" He shuts the door and we start across the street. "I love it!"

The place is packed and cocktail hour is in full swing. Wearing a dress was a good choice. This is the business crowd. The bands playing when we walk in. Cheye called his friend ahead of time to ensure that a table for two would be waiting for us. We sit down and the waiter comes to take our order. Cheye reaches over and grabs my hand. "Hey there, they'll be none of that." I pull my hand away. "Sorry, but I thought it was worth a try." Cheye orders a Scotch on the rocks. I get a Long Island ice tea.

The band is a quartet. The saxophone player is out front. He acknowledges us with a nod and gives Cheye a wink. Cheye winks back. "What's that all about?" Cheye looks at me innocently. "Oh, just a bet we made. I told Rizzo that I'm bringing the sexiest woman in Portland. I think he agrees." Cheye's determined to test where I stand with Omari.

"Hey Autumn!" I turn around to see Jerome, a colleague from work. Jerome hangs out at the bars after work to go "drag netting". After a few drinks, he becomes a social butterfly. Unfortunately, he doesn't care what his "catch of the day" looks like.

Letters to My Lover

Jerome is a gentleman. He specializes in older women with money, who are on the other side of their better days. "I'd like you to meet Cheye, he's a musician. Find a chair and join us." I notice that Cheye doesn't want anyone encroaching upon his territory.

"I'd love to Autumn, but I'm sitting with some clients. They're in from San Francisco, finishing the Peterson account. I just came over to say hello. A pleasure to meet you, Cheye."

The band plays for over an hour. When it's time for a break, no one wants them to stop. The saxophone player comes over and introduces himself. "Good evening, young lady, they call me Rizzo." He graciously extends his hand; I lay my hand within his. We don't shake, only touch.

Rizzo is a big, handsome brother, well over six feet tall. He obviously works out on a regular basis. His pullover shirt complements a good-looking upper body. "Good evening, my name is Autumn. Your music is delightful, thank you for sharing it with us." Rizzo slaps Cheye on the back. "How you doing, partner?" Cheye looks up. "The combination of good music, a fine woman, and a stiff drink, you know I'm in heaven!" We laugh. "You guys just sit back and relax, because it gets better!" Rizzo walks off and begins to mingle.

It's been a long day and my batteries are winding down. The two Long Island iced teas have given me a little buzz, which isn't helping me in the alert department. I touch Cheye on the shoulder, signaling my intention of leaving. "Looks like you're getting tired." He rubs my back. "Yeah, I think it's time."

We thank Rizzo one more time for the music and head towards the door. Looking disappointed that we're leaving so early, he holds the door open for us to exit. Cheye gives him another wink. Rizzo watches us with a certain curiosity as we leave the Cafe.

"Let me take five more minutes of your time and show you our office." Cheye wants the night to continue. Running across the street reminds me of the need to relieve myself of two Long Island iced teas. "Sure, but only if I can use your bathroom."

Cheye opens the door to his business suite. Its smart decor lends a warm feeling. "The bathroom is around the corner." He shuts

Perception and Reality

and locks the door behind us.

Looking in the mirror, my face looks tired. Splashing cold water, I try to revive myself for the ride home. I hear Cheye arranging things. He turns on the CD player. It's Will Downing. Oh no, romantic music!

Coming out of the bathroom, I realize that I'm behind closed doors with someone I really don't know. I immediately sense trouble. The look in Cheye's eye concerns me. He begins lighting candles.

"Come over here Autumn and give me a hug." I blush. My heart begins to race! "Cheye, I don't want to give you the wrong signal, so that's not a good idea." He comes closer. There *was* going to be trouble. He corners me, insisting on a hug. I push away, no longer receptive to his overtures. "Don't, Cheye!" He isn't listening. I break out in a sweat. He grabs me again, this time by the wrists. Holding my arms down by my sides, he begins to suck on my neck. Turning my head from side to side in disgust, I yell. "What the hell are you doing, let go of me!"

He steps back, but keeps a tight hold. "Come on, Autumn, I know why you called me!" All pretenses of being a gentleman are now gone. The real Cheye has me behind closed doors and is rapidly turning into Mr. Hyde. "Let go of me!" I jerk my arm away. "Look, Autumn, don't play games with me. We both know what you want and that's why you're here. Don't pretend to be something that you're not."

Grabbing me by the waist, he picks me up and body slams me to the carpet. The impact of hitting the floor, along with him landing on top, knocks the air out of me. I can't breathe or scream! He grabs my braids; it feels like he's trying to pull them out by the roots. He kisses me. His tooth hits my lip and I taste blood. Struggling to breathe, blood begins to fill my mouth. I spit up blood in his face.

He forces my legs apart. I can feel my dress tear. Regaining my senses, I realize that I'm being raped! No, I'm not going down like this, not like this! I start to scream at the top of my lungs. He tries to cover my mouth. I bite his hand. Blood is flowing everywhere. I continue to scream. "Shut the fuck up, bitch, and give me what I

Letters to My Lover

want!" His anger intensifies. "No," I scream! "Get of me! Get off me!"

Squeezing my legs together, I turn over onto my stomach, still screaming at the top of my lungs! "Help! Help!" Somehow, I'm able break some of his grip. We continue to wrestle on the floor. "Get off me! Get off me!" He punches me in the back of the head. "Bitch, you're gonna give me what I want!" I feel the punch, but I'm too numb to feel the pain.

In the background, I hear the buzzer ring. Someone's beating on the door. They shout, "Are you all right in there?" Again, I scream. "Help me, help me! Please help me!" I hear them trying to kick in the door. Realizing that someone is about to intrude, Cheye releases his grip. I kick him off me and run towards the door. It comes crashing in. It's Rizzo!

"What the hell's going on? What the...?" He sees my mouth bleeding. "Autumn, are you all right?" Rizzo rushes over and grabs Cheye by the throat, slamming him against the bookcase. "Are you crazy, mutherfucker? Are you crazy?" Rizzo doesn't know whether to help me or kill Cheye. He pushes him into the other room. I can hear Rizzo punch him repeatedly. "Mutherfucker, are you crazy?" Each time laying another blow on him.

Rizzo comes back into the room. I see the concern in his eyes. Struggling to breathe, I wipe my mouth. "Shit, Autumn, are you all right? Can you move?" It didn't feel like anything was broken, but I was becoming overwhelmed by the events. Rizzo leads me to the couch. "Let me get you a wet towel." He goes into the other room. This time, I can hear Cheye react as Rizzo walks by and kicks him. "Mutherfucker! You're lucky I don't kill you." He kicks him again.

Rizzo brings a towel and surveys the damage. He puts his arm around my shoulder. "Your lip is cut a little, but it's not bad. How do you feel?" I didn't know what to say. It's hard to believe what has just taken place is reality. I nod my head to reassure Rizzo that I'm all right. "Your dress is torn. Did he touch you?" Rizzo is genuinely concerned. It's if this scenario has happened before. "Don't worry, Autumn. You just relax. If that mutherfucker comes out of that room,

Perception and Reality

he's dead! Do you want me to call the cops?"

My head's in a spin. A half-hour ago, I sat listening to beautiful music, with someone I'd hope would be a friend. Now, I'm being asked if I want the cops to come and arrest the guy who beat me up and tried to rape me.

"I want to get out of here, Rizzo." Standing up, I try to rearrange my dress, along with my dignity. "I just want to go home." Rizzo hugs me, letting me know that no more harm would come to me. I hug him back and begin to cry in his arms. "What did I do to deserve this?" My lip bleeds on Rizzo's shirt.

"I'm not through with this mutherfucker yet, but I don't want you around for the rest of it. Do you think you can make it home okay?" He surveys the damage one more time. "What would've happened if you hadn't come along Rizzo?" He continues to hug me. "Luckily, I did Autumn. Now it's all over. Let me walk you to your car." The door has been kicked off its hinges. "Wait, there's one more thing." Rizzo goes into the other room and grabs Cheye's wallet. He takes out all the money. "He's giving you $200 dollars for another dress." Rizzo stuffs the money inside my purse. "Are you sure that you can make it home okay? The boys can handle the rest of the gig. I can drive you home if you want." I try to make the best of a bad situation. "I'm a big girl, Rizzo, I can make it."

The drive home is a nightmare. I'm numb. What's happened? My mind has quit working and I'm functioning on instinct. Time has stopped and I can't remember the sequence of events that have put me in such a bad place. My mouth stopped bleeding, but a lump has risen on the back of my head. Tears blind me. I must pull over. Dear God, what have I done to deserve this? What have I done? Guilt overwhelms me. My tears mix with the dried blood on my face.

I don't know how long I remained on the side of the road. I do remember thinking that I can't go home looking like this. I must pull myself together. Going into a convenience store to use the restroom, my torn, blood-spattered dress alarms the clerk. He keeps his eye on me the entire time I'm in the store. He must've mistake me for a crack-head. I emerge from the bathroom with enough composure to make it home.

    Walking into the house, I go directly to my room. Taking off my dress, I see bruises on my ribs. The cut on my lip isn't visible from the outside. My braids hide the lump on my head. Taking a deep breath, I realize that I've survived an attack that could have left me seriously injured or dead. "So this is what rape feels like."

    Taking off the rest of my clothes, I feel dirty. Remembering his anger makes me sick. I need to wash off the smell of his spit. Wanting to rid myself of everything that reminds me of this terrible night.

    The shower begins to wash away the humiliation of the evening. Staying under the shower until there is no more hot water, I feel drained. Sleep is all I want. My last thought before drifting off, is of waking up in the morning, hoping that I'd find this to be nothing more than a bad dream.

Chapter Thirty-Five
Thoughts of Loneliness

    Webster's dictionary describes loneliness as, *being by one's self, isolated, alone, one who avoids the company of others.*

    Living in the age of communication, with travel literally at our fingertips, why does loneliness dominate us? There are times when we can't get away from people, so why is loneliness so powerful? Loneliness...

    Like standing and waiting for a streetcar that never comes. People mill around, but don't look at one another. Why should I talk to anyone? Everyone wants *something*. What are they willing to do for me?

    Loneliness is the thing that haunts us the most on the inside. Ultimately, becoming our reflection. Like the shadow on a lamp-lit street corner, remaining in the abstract.

    I hear the musician and his song sounds so blue. His

Thoughts of Loneliness

expressions tell the story. I can relate to his song because it touches some place locked deep inside. At least he can describe his feelings.

Sometimes, I feel like the person who stands by the roadside with a sign saying, "Will work for food." The face tells the story; there's no need to talk, no need to explain. Loneliness is driving past and not acknowledging their plight exists.

Sometimes, when I look in the mirror, I hear the musician. I see the homeless person. I see the woman crying in her apartment, feeling meaningless, even to herself. Life's passing her by. I see the couple thrown together out of common fears, rather than mutual interest. Is loneliness tapping on my door? Let me look in the mirror.

I long to hear the musician play the tune that touches a special place in my heart. I long for someone's touch, so I can feel again. I long for a fleeting moment of joy, which will allow me to realize that I'm still human.

I am encased in solitude, helpless to control my own destiny.
Loneliness is shouting, but no one hears.
Loneliness is my constant companion.
Loneliness...

Chapter Thirty-Six
The Man's Dance

The single light cast a small circle upon the dark stage, highlighting the drums. Hamet walks slowly on stage, adorned from head to toe in African dress fit for a King. Paying homage to The Creator, he begins to weave a tapestry of sound; telling his story through the African drum. The fullness of the congas fill the theater with a sound so distinct, it's as if you could see the music. His drum calls out the first dancer, and with a run and leap, the strong, muscular dancer appears center stage. Hamet has called for "The Man's Dance," a dance that will demonstrate that there is none more powerful than the Mandingo man.

Letters to My Lover

Two more drummers join Hamet from opposite sides of the stage. Their drums talk to one another. The dancer interprets the drums and becomes a Gazelle. He performs a series of leaps that seem to defy gravity. The crowd takes notice.

Two dancers enter from opposite ends of the stage with a series of acrobatic flips, stopping in the middle. They eye each other as if to say, "I'm a better dancer than you." One performs a move as the other observes, figuring out how to best his competitor. The two men continue to duel each other, elevating the dance to another level. Finally, the first dancer steps in declaring their competition a draw. He raises both hands to the thunderous roar of an appreciative audience.

The rest of the troupe enters the stage from all directions, performing choreographed moves that amaze the audience. The men are dressed in loincloths and the sight of their sculpted bodies; performing feats usually reserved for professional athletes are a woman's delight. Each dancer steps to center stage, executing his finest move, trying to outperform the others. The women in the audience cheer for their favorite dancer. The drummers in the background continue to push the music to a fever pitch. The final dancer does a series of moves that displays the mastery over his body. The audience goes wild!

The men intertwine the music with their athletic abilities. This feast of music and dance spontaneously brings the crowd to its feet. Everyone roars with approval. Hamet signals the drummers and dancers to the finale. Within a split second, the drums hit their final beat and the dancers stop dead in their tracks.

These guys have pushed each other to their physical limits. The men begin taking their bows, one at a time. The women vote for their favorite dancer with seductive shouts. The dancers line up and bow to the drummers, showing their appreciation to the force behind their dancing. The audience continues their thunderous applause, as the entire troupe lines up to take a final bow. The audience begins shouting, "more, **more, bravo, bravo**"! The troupe takes another bow!

The Man's Dance

Suddenly, women begin to rush the stage, throwing their underwear at the feel of their favorite dancer! This scene is unreal. We break out laughing! Hamet signals the dancers with a drumbeat, to exit the stage. With one final high step, off we go!

That night, we got five curtain calls and a bunch of women wanting to come backstage, offering more than panties! Yes, dancing is my mistress and I will *always* love her!

Chapter Thirty-Seven
I Apologize

It's turning out to be a busy week at the office. Angela landed the basketball account, (along with the player) and we're trying to finalize the Memorandum of Understanding.

The phone rings. "Hello, Autumn, this is Rizzo. I called to find out how you're doing." Two weeks have passed since my world turned upside down. A nervous feeling swept through me. "Hello, Rizzo, thanks for calling." I take a deep breath. "I've picked up the pieces and decided to move on." There's a pause on the phone. "Good."

"Listen, there's someone here who has something to tell you." Rizzo put his hand over the phone's mouthpiece. I hear him say, "I think you owe this lady an apology." The next voice I hear is Cheye's.

"Autumn, I'm very sorry for disrespecting you in a most vulgar manner. What I did was wrong and I ask for your forgiveness."

Rizzo grabs the phone away from Cheye. "Autumn, I also apologize for my colleague's actions. Cheye received a generous dose of his own medicine. I guarantee you; he's learned a valuable lesson. You're a beautiful woman and worthy of the utmost respect. I hope this helps you close this door. Keep your head up, Autumn." I take another deep breath. "Thank you, Rizzo."

Rizzo's call is the highlight of a busy week. Since that terrible night, many emotions were swirling through my head. I felt them all, from guilt to hatred. However, Rizzo's compassion and concern for my well-being gave me hope.

That night, I went out and bought a new dress. I wore it to work the next day.

Chapter Thirty-Eight
Finding Stuff for The Big House

Omari's Letter:

Autumn,

I'm working on a few promising deals and scheduling a trip back to the Northwest, specifically to see you.

I met an interesting person at one of our dance performances. She came backstage to compliment our show and introduce herself. She's a retired missionary who spent twenty years living in Kenya. Her passion is collecting African art. I asked to see her collection and she obliged. Her collection contains *so many* beautiful pieces! Wanting to see more of her art, I kept visiting. One day she asks if I see anything that I like. I tell her, I love it all. She says that her kids don't appreciate the artwork. Describing the big house, I suggest that her beautiful collection would find a proper place in my home. Promising to keep her collection together, we struck a deal. Now I'm the proud owner of an art collection that took twenty years to assemble!

I also found a piece of American history in the form of some old tobacco-loading docks. Their construction dates back to the beginning of the 1800's and contains the history of southern America. These platforms were constructed of virgin-cut, old-growth hardwoods and used for over a hundred years. Not only did these platforms endure slavery days, they also survived the civil war, including General Sherman's march to the sea. Eventually they were dismantled and placed in a barn. The wood sat untouched for decades. I struck a deal with the old man that would bring new life to the wood.

Finding Stuff for The Big House

We worked together for weeks, selecting the choicest planks that met a particular specification for width and thickness. I took the planks to a lumberyard and milled it into hardwood flooring. We also milled enough wood to finish all the trim work. The beauty of this wood is unmatched and soon, the big house will contain one hundred and fifty years of American history.

I've also found some Italian marble. For transportation, I've rented a railroad car heading to Seattle. Leo's eagerly waiting for the materials to arrive. He's been doing some amazing things and I'm eager to see his progress.

The dance troupe is getting plenty of work and I'm in the best shape of my life. Anthony, one of the Atlanta dancers, is coming up to Seattle for a visit. He'll teach the "Man's Dance" to the guys.

I'll let you know of my schedule, as soon as it's complete. I eagerly look forward to seeing you.

Omari

Chapter Thirty-Nine
Back in the Great Northwest

I arranged my trip to Seattle but didn't tell anyone, except Leo and Autumn. Although I was taking a month off from work, there were more things to accomplish than there was time. It was best to come into town unannounced. Naturally, I wanted to see Autumn first, but knew how important it was to maximize my time at home and focus on some immediate priorities. I wanted to see Autumn, without any distractions.

I arrive in Seattle the same day as the train bringing the new materials. It's great seeing Leo again! When we start loading all of the goods onto the truck, Leo begins shouting with joy.

You see, Leo sparked my imagination like no other person;

Letters to My Lover

he inspired me to take bold chances. We knew each other's tastes and envisioned the same things. My surprise came when we arrived at the house. Leo's redesign of the house and gardens are breathtaking!

Leo brought in a bulldozer and cut fifteen-foot steps, traversing the hillside. Each step held a different type of garden. One contained strawberry and blueberry bushes and another step contained dwarf apples, cherry, plum and pear trees. A river rock waterfall cascades down the length of the hillside. The timbers used to lift the house were now stairs leading down winding paths. Leo also built a community vegetable garden big enough to feed the neighborhood. This mans ability to exercise his imagination made me proud.

Leo kept modifying the design of the house. He finished the third phase of the project; building the carriage house, along with adding the master bedroom suite in the main house. Leo joined the carriage house with the main house by building an atrium. The roof of the atrium is glass, allowing the natural light to flood the area. The atrium floor is finished with the bricks removed from the chimney, years earlier. Leo's design adds another two thousand square feet to the house. The big house now comprises twenty-two rooms and eight thousand square feet.

Walking through the house, I watch my dream unfold before me. My eyes are wide open. Every room is reconfigured. I listen in fascination, as Leo describes his thoughts regarding a particular idea. We both agree; the Italian marble will go into the kitchen and bathrooms.

It's difficult to find my way up to the second floor. Leo moved the stairs! Going up to the second floor, I walk directly into a panoramic view of Lake Washington! I walk into the bedrooms and realize that Leo has knocked down the walls separating the two rooms. Instead of four bedrooms on the second floor, there are two oversize ones. Leo also built in a set of French doors leading out to the covered decks on each bedroom. Adjoining the bedrooms is a sitting room facing the lake. The configuration of the bathroom on the second floor is unique. Each bedroom has its own private bathroom, with a toilet and vanity. Leo designed in a common shower room and Jacuzzi tub in-between the bathrooms. The shower room can hold six people

Back in the Great Northwest

comfortably and you can enter it from either side. He installed five showerheads, three of them coming out of the walls! Yes, the Italian marble is going to look great in this bathroom!

Going up the final flight of stairs, I walk into the thousand square feet, master bedroom. The vastness and the configuration of the room is evidence of Leo's artistic genius. Leo looks at me and says; "I'll be leaving soon, but I wanted to ensure my legacy. So, I designed and built this level of the house, especially for you brother. This is my gift to you!"

Wow, Leo! That's all I could say, wow!

Lora

It's a good idea coming into town unannounced. Lora was performing at the Bumbershoot festival and I wanted to get in as much music, in-between work, as possible. Anthony arrived from Atlanta the day prior and was eager to check out the Seattle music scene. Watching Lora perform on stage is a good start.

Lora's energy and cheerful expressiveness make her such a vibrant performer. I blow my whistle to accent her movements on the stage. Lora's eyes dance with excitement! By that sound, she knows that I'm watching her. She blows her whistle, returning my call. Blowing her whistle again, she dances off stage and into the audience. I've longed to see Lora dance and didn't want to disturb the moment, so I remain silent. Lora feels my energy and, spotting me from a distance, breaks into an African chant!

Lora comes over to me and begins to dance the "African Skirt Dance," a flirtatious dance. She knows I can't resist her charm. She wiggles her butt, enticing me to dance with her. I step into the male response, grabbing my "manhood," daring her to come closer. Soon, the audience surrounds us. Although it's been a year since we last danced, it could've been yesterday. Lora's spontaneity, her sense of rhythm and playfulness, her ability to read my mind and respond accordingly made our dancing special. I came to watch her dance but couldn't resist her charm and she knew that. She knew I'd jump at any chance to dance with her. Just to keep things fresh, I surprise

Letters to My Lover

Lora by calling Anthony over and we double-team her! We grab Lora by the waist and lifting her above our heads deposit her back on the stage. Lora blows her whistle one more time and dances off.

Lora wants to learn what we're doing in Atlanta. We dedicate a few days to working out and blend our dance routines together. The combination of African and urban dancing is spectacular!

Lora informs me of an abbreviated European tour, including a stop in France. She invites me to come along. It'll give us the chance to see Martinique and Marcel again.

Autumn

With my work complete, the remainder of my time is to be devoted to Autumn. I call her to let her know of my arrival the next day.

The drive to Portland is relaxing; it gives me time to unwind. Autumn comes running out of the house, greeting me with a kiss! It seems such a long time since we've seen one another. She looks as fine as ever and her warm embrace feels *so* good. We stand rapturously embracing for minutes! (Down, boy!)

Autumn arranged for us to stay at the house of an out-of-town girlfriend living on the Pacific Coast. That night, she prepares a special candlelight dinner. We have so many things to talk about that we stay up half the night getting reacquainted. Autumn looks radiant and I love holding her in my arms. We were both in dire need of an "oil change," and believe it or not, I've waited for my personal mechanic! (Passing up those out in five minutes- twenty-dollar jobs was tough.) I was proud to be able to control the "dawg" in me. This "dawg" liked eating out of his old bowl!

The feeling of waking up and seeing Autumn's face in the morning is wonderful. We spend a romantic day in bed, pampering each other. This particular place in time feels so right and this is where I want to be.

Our time on the beach is refreshing. We inhale the cool, refreshing, northwest breeze. Feeling the warmth of Autumn's body, I surrender to the moment.

Back in the Great Northwest

Sitting on the porch holding hands, we watch the horizon melt into the sea. "Autumn, our lives are so intertwined, they've become inseparable. You're a part of me now." Her soft eyes search my face. "What are you saying, Omari?" She knows the meaning of my words. "I want you near me." We sit in silence, still clasping hands.

The days pass quickly. It's difficult to accept that our time together is ending. At the airport, as I prepare to depart, we stand locked in an emotional embrace. Autumn is a strong woman, but for the first time, I see her cry. The final grasp of our hands remains framed in my mind. Slowly, we separate and I turn and walk away.

Chapter Forty
Breathless

The trip home excites me
Two ships in the night have become steady voyages
Autumn is more beautiful with time
And, she still leaves me breathless!

I love her passion
Funny, caring, considerate, thoughtful
Such a tender lover
Oh, how she leaves me breathless

Letters, phone calls, and stolen moments
Moving to Atlanta opened our eyes
Our time together, never long enough, our time apart, too long
Still, the thought of her leaves me breathless

She is wonderful
We've become closer with time
The "Mo better" makes us feel "Mo better."
All that lovemaking
Makes me breathless

Letters to My Lover

Our dreams become reality
My thoughts are of her
Soon we will be one
And I love
How she leaves me breathless

Chapter Forty-One
Let's Take the Plunge!

On the plane ride from Portland, I look out the window. The transition from snow-peaked mountains to the plains is breathtaking. I take in this beautiful scene and realize that my life is also in transition.

Sometimes, a man has no choice but to look in the mirror and admit the truth. The truth is that I'm in love. At thirty thousand feet, I was prepared to accept Autumn as my lifetime partner.

Dancing's taught me that timing is everything, and I could think of no better way of asking Autumn to marry me, than on one knee, under the Eiffel Tower, in Paris, France.

Omari's Letter:

Autumn,

One thing is clear; I miss you very much. I look forward to the time when we're living together in the big house. Then I can shout from the other room, "Hey Autumn, get me another beer!" (Burp!)

Lora's asked me to be part of an upcoming European tour. I've accepted her offer and want you to accompany us. Will you be my travel companion while we tour Europe? Please say yes.

Omari

Let's Take the Plunge!

Autumn's Reply:

Omari,

How can I resist such an invitation from a sexy man. I'd be delighted to be your travel companion. To be honest, I'd go to the ends of the earth with you! Let's take a picture at every border, like we did when we traveled across the States. Omari, you've made me the happiest woman in the world. I love you.

Autumn

Omari's comments:

With a verbal commitment in hand, I'm sitting on top of the world. I'm living a dream come true. It's difficult to imagine life evolving any better than the way things are heading. My professional career is going great and I'm making lots of money. My dance career is allowing me to travel the world, this time with Autumn by my side. The dream house is even coming along as scheduled!

Walking down the street, wearing a new suit, I'm feeling good. Love's hit me so hard, even the "dawg" has quit barking! About that time, a pretty woman in a Mercedes Benz drives by. With a little wave she shouts, "Looking good, baby!" Life doesn't get any better!

We finalize all of the arrangements for the Paris tour. Our schedules are a little different, so the band will arrive in Paris one day before Autumn. Everything's perfect.

Chapter Forty-Two
Paris Bound

Lora and the band fly from Seattle. Leaving out of Atlanta, we meet in New York and take the connecting flight to Paris.

Touring with Lora is always exciting. When I tell her of my intention to propose to Autumn, while in Paris, she thought I was joking. When I show her the diamond ring I'd brought along, she broke into a wedding song right on the airplane. Lora had witnessed so many of my escapades with other women. She knew Autumn had captured my heart.

Lora shows the ring to the other members of the band. During the rest of the trip, everyone dreams up exotic scenarios of how I should propose. Deciding that everyone will be involved, we'll perform a special dance at the base of the Eiffel Tower. The finale of the dance will have me asking for Autumn's hand in marriage.

Our dear friend Marcel, couldn't be at the airport to greet us, he was occupied hosting an Egyptian delegation. He arranged for everyone to meet at his house for dinner that evening and left special instructions for me to invite Martinique. Before going to sleep, I call Martinique and invite her to Marcel's dinner party. It's nice to hear her voice.

Martinique

The phone rings at 4:00 p.m.; Martinique's sexy voice is on the other end. "This is your wake-up call." She's attending an art opening and wants me to be her escort.

Dinner at Marcel's starts at 9:00 p.m. Autumn is leaving New York on the evening flight; I'll pick her up at the airport in the morning. Everything is in order.

When Martinique steps into the lobby of the hotel, my heart skips a beat. This woman is beautiful! It's been two years since our meeting; yet, it's as if time has stood still. We embrace. The memory of our last encounter dances in our head. "Martinique, it's so nice to

Paris Bound

see you again." We continue to hug. "I'm so glad you called, Omari." I hold her close, wanting her to feel my strength. She giggles and brushes my cheek with her perfect lips. "My friend's having his opening, that'll give us time to talk. I want you to tell me everything going on in your life." Martinique is bubbling with energy. Grabbing my hand, she lets me know that I'm her captive audience. The valet opens the door to the taxi and off we go.

At the party, we toast one another. "To our meeting again." She looks me deep in the eyes. "Omari, you look very content and happy. You're in love, yes?" I return her gaze. "Yes I am Martinique. Would you like to meet her?"

Martinique, there's something I must tell you. There's something about you that I can't resist. Your style and grace make you unforgettable. I can't deny my attraction to you." She squeezes my hand. "Omari, we'll always have our special place in time. I still remember the magic we made. You're a unique person and I love that you've come back into my life. Let there be no secrets between us and we'll always remain friends." With those words, we touch glasses and take a sip of wine. I can't resist giving Martinique another kiss. The moment takes us back in time.

When will I meet this lady who's captured your heart?" Martinique circles the rim of her wineglass with her manicured nail. "She'll be arriving tomorrow morning, on TWA flight 800 out of New York. I'm meeting her in the airport at 9:00 am. Until then Martinique, here's where I want to be. I want to be with you." We touch glasses again. Martinique whispers softly to herself, "C'est la vie!" I didn't understand, but I understood. (Such is life.)

The artwork is beautiful. Martinique introduces me to the artist, Francisco. He's a playful person who's had a little too much to drink. Speaking French, he compliments Martinique on her good taste in art and men. They laugh. I invite him to our show the next evening at the Riviera Club. He accepts, after Martinique insists that he see the act. Soon after, she excuses us from the party. We stroll along Jazz Alley and listen to the music on our way to dinner.

Seeing Martinique again is another dream come true. Her

Letters to My Lover

stunning beauty and her sophistication attract me. I realize that most women wouldn't understand our attraction for one another transcends jealousy. We both know, in some way, our souls are connected; yet, we understand the finality of the evening.

Holding hands, we walk by as the sax man blows his tune. If we could stop time. If only we didn't live a continent away, life may have taken a different turn. With the saxophone setting a mellow mood, we stop, embrace, and exchange a long passionate French kiss.

Marcel

We arrive at Marcel's house as the Egyptian delegation is exiting the limousine. Walking in behind them, Marcel greets us at the door.

"Omari! Talking about a sight for sore eyes!" We give each other a big hug, trying to squeeze the breath out of one another. "Marcel you look wonderful!" Without missing a beat, he glances in the mirror behind us, "You're right, I do!" Everyone laughs. "And you brought Martinique!" They greet each other with a kiss. "Martinique, I see that life's treating you well. It must be, if you're still running around with this character." Martinique uses her sexy eyes. "Marcel, any time spent with you is a blessing." She kisses him again, this time on the lips. "Omari, I hope you don't mind if we share this beautiful woman tonight!"

Lora and the rest of the band show up a few minutes later. Watching Lora enter a room is always a magnificent moment and she didn't disappoint. Wearing an African ceremonial dress with a matching headdress, she is beautiful! This woman *is* a Queen in every sense of the word. Marcel kisses her hand, acknowledging her regal beauty. The rest of the Egyptian delegation line up to greet this woman as if she *were* a Queen.

"Martinique, look at you! It's good to see you again. How are you?" Lora draws Martinique near, they exchange kisses on the cheek. "Lora, it's so nice to see you again, and thank you for bringing this man back to Paris."

Paris Bound

Marcel's dinner parties, and his mix of people, are always a joyful event. He asks us to kick off the evening by singing the African greeting song we sang at our initial meeting, two years earlier. Lora asks the band to stand; we accompany her as she dedicates the song to Marcel's dinner guests. The harmony of the music and the joyful event make for a special moment. We turn to our Egyptian guests for the first chorus and face Marcel for the second.

It's nice to be amongst old friends and new ones. I sit in a moment of reflective silence; again realizing how far dancing has taken me. This is it, the pinnacle of my life, and it's only going to get better with Autumn's arrival in the morning. I'm sitting on top of the world and savoring every moment, *knowing* that life hasn't denied me.

Dinner is wonderful and the cross-cultural conversation is delightful. Marcel insists that Lora sit across from him, so he can admire her beauty.

Marcel brings out the pictures taken at our United Nations performance two years earlier. The photos bring back memories and reinvigorate my feelings for Martinique. "These copies are for you Omari," Marcel remarks. "Thank you, my dear friend. They'll be added to my collection, and when I am too old to dance, I'll pull out these memories and relive my youth." Marcel brings out one of Lora; it's matted and framed. "For you, my beautiful Queen." He presents it to her with a kiss.

Marcel ushers us into the living room to enjoy his lovely view of downtown Paris. Martinique asks if she can play the baby grand piano in the corner. Everyone nods in approval. She sits and runs her fingers over the keys. Looking over at me, she closes her eyes and begins to sing. "For all we know. We may never meet again. So, before we go, let's make this moment sweet again. We won't say goodnight until the last minute. I'll hold out my hands and my heart will be in it… For all we know…"

Lora looks over at me. She knows I've told Martinique about Autumn. Martinique plays beautifully. Putting the crowning touch to an evening no one will forget. An evening spent surrounded by friends from the neighborhood and friends from the other side of the world.

Letters to My Lover

Chapter Forty-Three
We Have Breaking News

It's 2:00 in the morning when the phone rings. Marcel looks stunned that anyone would call at such a late hour. "Marcel, you must turn on the news, there's been a terrible accident." The caller's voice conveys urgency. "Please turn on the news."

"We have breaking news from CNN. You are looking at the first pieces of debris that have been picked up by the search and rescue ships from TWA flight 800, bound from New York to Paris. TWA flight 800 erupted into flames shortly after takeoff, around 9:00 p.m. from JFK airport in New York. There are no known survivors. Coast Guard and Navy search and rescue efforts are continuing at this moment, even as jet fuel burns on the ocean surface. Authorities are not optimistic of finding anyone alive from the ill-fated flight. All two hundred and eighty seven passengers are feared dead. Among the travelers: a class of forty students and four teachers from Jonathan Alder High School in Columbus, Ohio, en route to Paris on a field trip. Authorities from the National Transportation Safety Board and the Federal Bureau of Investigation have arrived at JFK to begin the initial investigation. Eyewitnesses at the airport, as well as Long Island residents, report seeing the plane explode. Other aircraft in the area reported seeing TWA flight 800 burst into flames. Air traffic controllers are trying to corroborate these eyewitness accounts. After the explosion, debris apparently rained into the Atlantic Ocean over several miles. However, authorities are cautious regarding verifying these accounts, believing they'll learn more and gather more debris when daylight arrives. We'll have more on this story, as details become available. This is CNN reporting."

Marcel's anguished eyes meet mine. "Come on, Omari, we've got to get to the airport!"

We Have Breaking News

At the Airport:

We listen to the car radio on our way to Charles de Gaulle Airport. My mind can't grasp the gravity of the situation.

The privilege of having a diplomatic pass and parking in front of any building doesn't strike me as important anymore. You see, death believes in equal opportunity for all. We step out of the car, sensing the fear and trepidation in the air.

Frantic inquires from loved ones add to the confusion at the airport. Slowly I begin to understand that I no longer need to be at the airport at 9:00 a.m. to pick up Autumn. There'd be no airplane arriving. What didn't register is that Autumn has died.

Confused thoughts swirl through my mind. Maybe she missed the flight. I picture Autumn still in New York City, silently complaining about being stuck in the airport all night long.

Slowly, the reality of the moment begins to sink in. Starting in my throat, it strangles me until I can't speak. Working its way into my chest, I can't breathe. Soon, it feels as if someone has climbed upon my shoulders and I have to sit. I'm disoriented and sinking. Marcel repeatedly asks me if I'm all right. Then, everything becomes a blur.

Watching the sunrise took on a different meaning now. Strangely, my watching the sunrise with Martinique years ago flashes through my mind. Maybe the thought is meant to give me enough relief to endure the pain engulfing me from all sides. We visit the TWA Operations Office for official word from the airline. It's confirmed; Autumn's name was on the passenger manifest. The agony of hanging around the airport, waiting for bad news, adds to the misery of the moment. The glare of the television cameras, violating every aspect of decency, in order to publicize our grief, pushes me into another reality. Outside, a TV crew shouts questions. "How do you feel?" They make me a reluctant witness, by filling me in on the details of Autumn's demise. This deepens my detachment from reality. I'm not here anymore. I don't know where I am. I barely hear Marcel saying, "Hang in there, Omari, hang in there." (The referee continues his count, "eight, nine, and ten. You're out!")

Letters to My Lover

Chapter Forty-Four
Three Weeks Later - Omari's Thoughts

It's been three weeks since my final night in Paris. TWA officials put me on a plane the following day and were there to greet me back in the States. I apologize to the band for having to leave; Lora was very concerned.

Later that day, I spoke with Autumn's parents. I didn't know what to say. My inviting their daughter to Paris had caused her demise. There's mostly silence on both ends of the line. We realize that nothing any of us can say will change the outcome. I thought it important to tell them of my intention to ask for Autumn's hand in marriage. There's a pause on the phone before Autumn's mother replies, "I speak for my daughter when I tell you Autumn loved you with all of her heart. I remember her excitement as she left for vacation. I remember her describing how happy she was to have met and fallen in love with you. Omari, we look at you as our son. Although it's difficult to know what tomorrow will bring, when you're ready, let us hear back from you."

Climbing the Hill

After two months, I still find it difficult to express these vast arrays of emotions. Inexplicable things register in my mind at odd times. I feel what part of Billie Holiday's heart in which she sings. I realize how Miles could play so bitter, yet so sweet. I've always loved the music, but now I felt the essence of the blues.

Martin Luther King stated, "The true measure of a man is not what he does in times of comfort and contentment. The true measure of a man is what he does in times of uncertainty and confrontation." This experience revealed the essence of my soul. That exploration allowed me to pick up the shattered pieces and slowly begin the process of moving forward. Some of my emotions, I'm not proud of. However, I must be honest with myself and to The Creator. I must acknowledge all of my thoughts and deal with them as best I know how.

During my headlong dive into madness and the slow ascension

Three Weeks Later - Omari's Thoughts

back, I cursed The Creator. I cursed God because I didn't understand why God was so cruel to me. I cursed God because God had revealed a taste of heaven and I'd become addicted. I cursed God, not for Autumn's death, but for not allowing me the opportunity for closure. When Autumn died, my heart was ripped out of me as violently as having my teeth extracted with a set of pliers. A piece of my soul went with her. After I regained *some* of my senses, I felt ashamed, yet, at the time, the thoughts were *very* real. In my deepest and darkest hour, The Creator provided me with a ray of hope.

  I recall an episode in the Army, which propelled me from adolescence into manhood. On a forced march, our platoon walked twenty miles with full backpacks. A week before, a bully soldier was harassing a smaller soldier in the platoon, one being no match for the other. When the platoon came to an eleven-mile hill, we knew we were in for a true test of our manhood. This hill told no lies. It stood in front of us and defied us to conquer it.

  One-third of the way up the hill, the weak began to drop behind. Halfway up, the bully soldier starts crying, saying he couldn't make it. I remember going within myself to find the strength to continue. I remember thinking out of self-preservation of only the next step. I remember my nose starting to bleed and doubting my own limitations. I also remember deciding that I'd rather die than quit. This hill displayed my character, stripped down to its bare essentials, and my character didn't quit.

  The next memory is of sitting at the top of the hill, having conquered it, bloody and exhausted. I gave thanks to The Creator for providing me the strength to endure. That was my passage into manhood. From that memory, I realized that I was walking another hill in life and there'd be many more.

  The nice thing about closing one chapter is that it signals the beginning of another. I was ready to turn the page.

Letters to My Lover

Giving Back

Having felt that I'd performed admirably for the corporation, I wanted them to return the favor. Sitting down one day, I wrote a proposal, suggesting that a one-year sabbatical, performing community service was a good public relations initiative. Two weeks later, with one hundred thousand corporate dollars to spend, I received my walking papers for a year. (I quit cursing The Creator and became grateful again.)

The concept of healing my soul grew in significance over the next year. I remember complaining one day about a foot injury sustained while dancing. The next day, I met a man who had no legs. I quit complaining about paying high rent when I witnessed a homeless mother sleeping in a car with her children. I saw a woman with two infants trying to catch the bus and could see her dilemma. Never again would I criticize anyone for having too many kids. Offering a ride was a better solution. This personal journey provided me the opportunity to observe life though other people's eyes and performing random acts of kindness awakened my senses, along with my sensibilities.

During this sabbatical, I thought I was to give service to my people, but I received so much more in return. James Baldwin stated, "The quality of our lives is best determined by the people and personalities that we meet along the way." Slowly, I could feel myself waking up.

Leo's letter to Omari:

Omari

It's been a while since I've heard from you. I thought it wise to write. I'll be leaving soon and it's time for us to figure out our next step. Omari, the big house is ready for its owner. It would be inappropriate to allow anyone else but you to christen its new beginning. Think about coming home.

Undoubtedly, you are still suffering, but always remember my

Three Weeks Later - Omari's Thoughts

friend, through the ashes of destruction, are sewn seeds of hope. Take a road trip and see some of your friends.

One thing is certain; rebuilding the big house has been an adventure of a lifetime. It's going to be difficult to find anything that will top this, but I'm gonna try!

Leo

Chapter Forty-Five
Going Home

Almost a year has passed since Autumn's death. Leo was right, it *was* time to go home, and seeing my friends *was* a good idea. I made a few phone calls to my colleagues in Seattle and managed to secure an assignment starting in six weeks.

With my walking papers in hand, it's time to bid farewell to a beautiful place. Leaving Atlanta is difficult. I've grown accustomed to the weather, the food, the dancing and being surrounded by beautiful Black people. Leaving the outskirts of Atlanta, I look back one more time to see the beautiful skyline. *I'm breathless.*

On the road and feeling the engine vibrate throughout my body, relaxes me. My friends know of the tragedy, and as I drive, I try to prepare myself for the inevitable questions. I'm eager to see my friends but don't want to open old wounds.

My first stop is to visit my friend Vicki, living in Houston. Little has changed since our last visit (except for our waist sizes). Her wit always captivates me and her crazy energy is a blessing. Over dinner, she brings out all of the pictures we've taken together. "Omari, I remember when you couldn't dance a lick!" We laugh so hard, tears stream down our faces! It feels good to laugh. It feels good to be in the company of friends and to celebrate life. Seeing Vicki helps put a few pieces of the puzzle together. Nuances of my former self begin to emerge from a long, dark sleep.

Letters to My Lover

Driving across the Texas and New Mexico plains reveals the emptiness remaining within certain parts of my soul. I stop in the middle of nowhere and watch the sunset melt into the plains, feeling at home, surrounded by this emptiness. Taking out my sleeping bag, I sleep beneath the stars.

The next morning, I continue to drive. On the distant horizon, I see the mountains sprout from the earth. By evening, I'll be in Southern California and have made plans to see my friend Tshlene. Weaving through the traffic, I make my way to Compton. Pulling into the driveway, I honk, signaling my arrival.

Seeing Tshlene rush out the door brings on another emotional wave. She hugs me tight and I feel her warmth. I try to let go but she pulls me tighter, refusing to let me hide the rebirth of my emotions. We remain in our embrace for minutes. I begin weeping in her arms. She comforts me with her gentle words of reassurance that everything is all right. I can feel myself waking up out of this long dark sleep and it feels good.

I stay in LA for a few days, hanging out with my twin brother. He's playing with some of the best musicians in the town. My brother and the music are the perfect combination. It's been a long time since Tshlene and I have danced together. Now, it feels like ten years earlier, when we first met. We dance as if there is no tomorrow, only the moment.

Tshlene and I spend an evening talking. Ever so slowly, she peels away the layers of my resistance and encourages me to talk about Autumn.

Images flash through my mind with a perfect sense of order. It's as if many of my experiences have been pre-ordained. Insight floods my mind and the burden of carrying around some un-understandable thing lifts from my shoulders.

Autumn introduced me to something very simple called love. Autumn introduced me to undeniable, unstoppable, uncompromising, compassionate love. It's difficult to feel sad because I'd found the all-elusive component we all search for in our lives. I'd found love.

Leaving LA, I take scenic Highway 101, going north. Stopping

Going Home

in Carmel to buy postcards, I roll out my sleeping bag on Pebble Beach to write my friends, giving a new address. The sun feels warm hitting my face. I listen to the surf pound the beach.

> On the beach, I sit
> And this is where I slept
> I woke up in the night, thinking of you
> Or, because my ass was getting wet!

Omari's new address: 6128 South Pilgrim Street, Seattle, WA 98118

San Francisco is the next port of call, to visit my friend Tom. His sense of humor was somewhat sick and his one-liners never stopped. You never knew what to expect. Our paths had crossed years earlier at a comedy club. He was the act and I was the heckler. It turned out to be the funniest part of the show. You couldn't help but admire someone brave enough to let his unadulterated humor risk him bodily harm.

"Maybe it's a blessing that you remain single, Omari. I'd hate to see some kid come out with a head shaped like yours. He'd grow up tough because everyone in grade school would be "Jones-ing" him until he grew into that big "thang"!

Sonoma Valley and a trip through the wine country are next. This gives me an excuse to replenish my wine collection (which has dwindled down to a half bottle of the twist-off cap variety). Ten vineyards and five hundred dollars later, I'm sporting two cases of the "good stuff". Wine guaranteed to pop the panties off the most sophisticated woman! Actually, most of the sophisticated women I knew would settle for a twenty-dollar bill and a ride back to the corner. (Yes, Tom rubbed off on me in the worst way.)

My next stop is the Sequoia National Forest, where I lose myself in nature. The redwood trees stand hundreds of feet high and engulf me in their grandeur. Entering Humboldt County is like stepping back twenty years in time. The last of the hippies have settled here. They're having a beach party, but everyone knows that a party isn't a party, unless you have some Black people in the mix. I offer my services (for a small fee of course). So, here I am, in front of a beach

Letters to My Lover

fire, watching the sunset, sitting beside people with names like "Heaven" and "Virtue," feeling overdressed because my clothes match.

The weather cooperates during the entire trip. I repeatedly pull over to watch the wave's crash against the rocks and remember the perfect times Autumn and I spent on the ocean. As I reminisce, I'm torn between fond memories of the past and living for today.

Traveling through Oregon, I battle with the thought of visiting Autumn's parents. I drive almost to their block, but can't summon enough courage to go around the corner and knock on the door. I feel confused. The knot in my throat is so tight; I couldn't have spoken even if I did knock on the door. I stay in Portland that evening, but the memories of the past haunt me all night long. I can't rest and I wake up the next morning in a pool of sweat, feeling as if I've run a marathon. Dancing taught me the importance of timing, and something didn't feel right about bringing back such painful memories, so I didn't.

It's on to my final destination, Seattle. I drive by Fort Lewis, the Army port-of-call that brought me to the Northwest. In the distance is Mount Rainier, the attraction that kept me here for so many years. Soon, Seattle appears on the horizon. I feel a tear in my eye because I know that I'll soon be home.

Driving up to the house, I realize that my journey of two years has ended. I sit in the car for a few minutes, numb from the adventure of traveling across the country. I bow my head and thank The Creator for keeping me safe. I ask for forgiveness for doubting the existence of a supreme being in my time of weakness. The feeling of living enough experiences for a lifetime overwhelms me as I emerge from the car.

I'm home. I know that when I open the door, a flood of memories will fill my head. They'll be as real as the present moment. I open the door, and they do.

Chapter Forty-Six
Completing The Big House

It's difficult to imagine how far the house has evolved through the years of construction. I recollect the sacrifice and imagination it took to build. Yet, after so many years, the sacrifice has lost its edge. I walk through the house and remember all of the personalities who came through, realizing that it was impossible for them to envision what Leo and I saw. I gaze in amazement at how far our dream drove us. I also realize that this was an obsession.

Leo left me with a dream come true. I've come to realize how much I miss Leo. I miss his laughter. I miss his cooking. I miss the smell of marijuana lingering around the house. But most of all, I miss his creative energy.

We're Done!

Within a month of my coming home, the house makes its final transformation into a polished diamond. The hardwood floors are beautiful. The windows, encased in wood trim, are a fine work of art. The porch is an enclosed sun-room, framing a spectacular Lake Washington view. The kitchen floors and countertops are Italian marble. The living and dining rooms display a simplistic, yet spatial quality. African artwork adorns every wall throughout the house, giving a feeling of being in a museum. Every room has its own unique feature and as I walk through the house, every picture tells a story.

Leo made an architectural statement in designing the penthouse suite. He succeeded beyond his wildest dreams. To be in this space *is* a spiritual experience. It defines our dream. Our dream *is* reality, and I stand savoring the moment.

In honor of Leo's uncompromising dream, I rename the big house "Leo Manor". Thank you so much, brother. I love you.

Letters to My Lover

Chapter Forty-Seven
A New Beginning

    Five weeks to the day after returning to Seattle, the big house is officially complete. The morning sun shines through the windows of the master bedroom suite. Everything is *so* beautiful. Flotillas of boats sit on the lake, against the background of snow-capped mountains. I linger in bed, realizing that my dream, five years in the making, is now reality. I reminisce about the many experiences and realize that building this house *was* a labor of love.

    Later, during the day, I go outside to water the plants. The water sprays into the sun, creating a colorful rainbow. At the end of the rainbow stands Autumn, in all of her radiant beauty. She's smiling, as she always did. I can't believe what I see, yet, it feels so real! I start walking towards her, and in an instant, the rainbow, along with Autumn disappear. I sure do miss that woman.

    On this day, I realize how blessed my life has been. Knowing that I've danced before kings of countries is a great honor. Yet, with all of these experiences, I know that crossing paths with Autumn and falling in love, is the brightest moment in my life.

Omari's Final Letter:

My Dearest Autumn

    It's important that I take the time to tell you how wonderful it was meeting you. You brought a very special element into my life and you taught me to appreciate every moment. You gave your love unconditionally, and for that, I'm eternally grateful.

    I've acquired a profound appreciation of life because of you. Reminiscing about our time together always brings pleasant memories (and a pencil in my pocket). Finishing our chapter within the book of life encourages me to begin the next.

    Autumn, I've taken the time to grieve, and with this letter, I hope to find closure. I know someday, somewhere, our spirits will meet again, laugh again, embrace again, and love again. I look forward

A New Beginning

to that time.
> Autumn, I'll always love you.

Omari
(Letter never sent)

Chapter Forty-Eight
Back to Reality

I'd been sitting beside the box reading letters all day. They lay all around me, one after another, still in order. Ten years have passed since my introduction to Autumn. Reading our letters made it seem like yesterday.

My dancing career ended two years ago. I graciously elected to retire my shoes, rather than go out like an old boxer, not knowing when to quit. My last performance was dancing with Lora at the World Arts and Dance Festival in Redmond, Washington.

One of my friends suggested that I turn Leo Manor into a bed and breakfast. We call it "Leo's Hideaway". We began offering Seattle vacation packages. Soon, we were greeting visitors from all parts of the world. Two memorable visitors came from France. They were Martinique and Marcel. I remember having to leave suddenly during our last encounter and missing the opportunity to dance for them. They received deluxe accommodations at "Leo's Hideaway," along with front row tickets to see my final dance performance with Lora. It was such a joyful occasion. Our final performance turned out to be our finest!

Leo's continues traveling the world. He sends an occasional post card, letting me know that I'm with him in spirit.

Things have worked out pretty well for me and at the ripe old age of forty-five, I retired from the corporation. One day, I'm going to sit down and write about some of my adventures.

Letters to My Lover

ABOUT THE AUTHOR

"Letters to My Lover" is Kevin Howard's debut novel.

"The inspiration for this novel originated from reading an excerpt from my diary, written exactly ten years earlier. That ability to go back and to relive a precise 'slice in time' was a revelation, for in those writings were talk of the future. Reaching a time of 'transformation wisdom' within life prompted me to sit down and reflect upon my experiences. I found the reflection to be a joyful, insightful, liberating and wonderful experience."

Kevin's interests are wide ranging. Kevin's been associated with the aerospace industry for twenty years. He's also built a composite experimental airplane and is currently involved with the deployment of the International Space Station.

The Victorian mansion written into the story is a real life experience which began in 1986 and completed in 1996.

Kevin began dancing, when his brothers started organizing bands and playing locally in the late 60's and 70's. He's developed a *unique* style of dance with its origins in Urban, African, Latin, Soul, and Funk.

We're interested in hearing your thoughts about this novel, so please share with us your opinion.

Kevin Howard 6128 South Pilgrim Street, Seattle, WA 98118
Africandance@Yahoo.com
www.blackstar-media.com/Africandance